Of Talons & Steel

Sam Thorne

Content Warning

While a work of fiction, this novel contains material some may find disturbing. These can be found listed below.

Body horror
Misgendering
Death
Blood
Violence
Homophobia
Transphobia
Dysphoria
Abduction

Table of Contents

Chapter One

The trees cast a shifting blanket of shadows over the waves crashing into the base of the cliffs. Tucking her wings close, Xellen dropped the last several yards to the knoll and crouched to make herself as small as possible. Cocking her head, she listened for any sign she had been spotted. The pines creaked and rustled around her, and the familiar, endless crash and roar of the sea below soothed her nerves.

Assured she was alone, Xellen crept forward through the brush, hissing as branches snagged in her curls and sharp stones bit into her palms and bare feet. Fortunately, it wasn't far before the copse of trees opened to a panoramic view of the village below, nestled against the sea and bathed in inky darkness.

Night after night, she had sought different perches from which she could see the village, trying to catch a glimpse of the knight who patrolled the streets every night. She'd seen him once at the morning toll, just as the sun began to crest the distant horizon, and she and her flock returned to their rock from early hunting. A flash of golden hair.

It was only a phantom from her past haunting her. Nothing more. Yet she couldn't help but want to *know*. To be sure. It seemed impossible, though. It was only safe to come on moonless nights, when the humans below couldn't see her, but neither could she see the spectral figure who haunted the hole in her heart.

A snap and crash not far behind her caused Xellen to whip her head around, the feathers along her neck and back prickling with anxiety. She was no longer alone.

Digging her talons into the loose rock and dirt, she leapt upwards, and beat her winged arms, climbing along the treeline.

"Now!" someone shouted, and something heavy twisted over one of her legs.

Xellen let out a startled shriek at the unexpected weight of a bola, flapping hard to keep from plummeting, when a second one wrapped around a wing. Kicking and lashing out with her talons, she spiraled to the ground.

"Pin it, quickly!" the same voice barked, and four shadowy figures rose up from amongst the planted rows, shedding grassy blankets.

She kicked at the binding on her leg, clawing at the second one pinning her wing with a shriek of frustration, but the men were on her in an instant, all grasping, tearing hands. She twisted beneath them, lashing out with her free leg. Her talons tore through fabric and flesh and a man went down screaming, his hands feebly grasping his belly as blood and offal spilled out.

"Fuck!" a man bellowed above her, snatching a fistful of her head feathers so tightly she felt the pins try to pull from her skin. "Rope! Now!"

Xellen screeched, trying to kick at the one holding her feathers. Before she could lift her leg, another hand pushed down on her back.

"Here, here, take it!" one of the men said frantically. "Careful! Watch its legs!"

She reached up for the hand in her feathers, catching the wrist with the long nails on her fingers.

"Its hand! Get its—"

Her hand was pried from his, but she felt skin under her nails catch, tearing, before her arm was wrenched up behind her back until her shoulder burned. Her screech bled into a crying scream.

"Damn it, don't break its wings!"

Her other arm was pinned to her back and her wrists were quickly tied with rough rope. Somehow, she got one knee under her amidst all the struggling and tried to surge upright. She could only get one lumbering step forward before two sets of hands pushed her down onto her knees and shoved her head down against the dirt, feathers tearing free in their hands.

"Get the muzzle before it can get a finger!"

A hard mask of leather was shoved roughly against

her mouth and chin, pinching against the bottom of her nose and digging into her cheeks. Buckles were pulled tight around the back of her head. One man held her shoulders down while the other moved to her feet, yanking them together and wrapping something rough around her ankles. She flexed her talons, but could not stretch them through what felt like burlap. Then more rope, holding the fabric in place.

Then they all rushed back, leaving Xellen immobile on the ground. She gasped through the tiny holes in the leather mask and yanked at her arms and legs, trying to get anything free.

This couldn't be happening. She'd been so careful. She'd always been careful.

A hard boot nudged under her waist and shoved her onto her back. Xellen shrank against the ground as three men leered over her. The one she had struck was nearby, motionless, possibly dead. And a fifth man approached, his face sharply angled in the moonlight, wearing a cruel expression.

"Look at *her*," one of the three men said luridly. "I'd heard they had breasts, but I never thought—"

"Oh, you wanna fuck it?" Another laughed, jabbing his thumb at the fifth man. "You'll have to ask Remo."

"And get my cock torn off? Hell no."

"Then you had better get her in the wagon," snapped Remo, jerking his head toward something Xellen had assumed was some piece of farm equipment in the dark.

Two of the men grabbed her, one on each of her

arms, and dragged her backwards. Xellen tried to yank herself free the whole way to what was more of a cage than a wagon. She was hoisted up and shoved inside onto a thick bed of straw that pricked against the soft skin of her belly and chest. Xellen rolled onto her side and heaved upright as the cage door slammed in front of her, and she landed roughly against it.

Raucous laughter broke out, and Xellen sank down against the straw, swallowing a terrified sob. Her muscles were spent and tired, with barely enough strength to tuck her knees close to her chest.

"All right, Remo, we got it! Cage is secured. Another beastie off the wish list for the lord."

"Good. You and Leon take it to the camp. Make sure to keep a guard on it at all times. I don't want it escaping. We'll tend to Santo."

"Let's go!"

The wagon lurched, and Xellen braced herself as it bounced and rolled against the terrain, heading for the road, then following it inland. Away from the shore. Away from her flock. She'd fallen into a trap, and there was no one to save her.

Chapter Two

They were getting closer.

Orelia watched the winged shapes wheel and dive for fish out beyond the breakers, barely more than grey smudges in the pink dawn, too big to be birds. She'd watched the harpies hunt every sunrise and sunset since her conroi had been sent out to the small fishing village of Tamini—a small pleasure in the otherwise dull repetition of long, quiet patrols and meals taken alone.

It was tedious, boring work. Everything about her knighthood had been tedious and boring once she had clawed her way out of squiredom. She almost missed the rigors of training and practice combat as a squire at the Crown's city, if it weren't for all the rest that had come with it. Compared to that, tedium was a blessing.

It could be far worse, she consoled herself whenever she found herself chewing on dissatisfaction. Patrolling a fishing village along the border was as much a part of knighthood as charging into battle. Vigilance, her mentor would say. She vigilantly hoped they would not be lingering in the village much longer.

Below, in the village nestled between hills, a bell rang, signaling all the fishermen had returned safe from their early morning trip and an end to Orelia's night patrol.

With a low groan of not quite relief, Orelia got to her feet, stretching her sore, stiff muscles. It was a small favor Remo had decided they were only to wear their gambesons, and not their armor on patrol, as was demanded in training.

With a fond pat of the old, grey cypress stump that served faithfully as her seat, Orelia set off down the winding footpath back to the village, eager to reach her bunk and steal an hour to read before sleep. It was a trifling thing, and gods forbid any of the other knights caught on to what sort of story it was, but she looked forward to it more than anything else in what had become listlessly long days and nights.

"Agnolo!"

Orelia snapped from her wistful thoughts of reclining in bed reading. Opening and closing her fists, she took a slow breath before she turned to face her Knight Commander. "Yes?"

He glowered up at her, the hand at his sword tightening visibly. "Where have you been? The bell has been ringing."

"Patrolling. Per your orders, ser."

The corner of Remo's mouth twitched beneath the carefully groomed black hairs of his mustache. "Is that cheek I hear?"

His voice had gone soft, and Orelia knew she was in dangerous territory. She straightened, folding her hands at her back so she stood at proper attention before she answered. "No, ser."

His eyes narrowed, and Orelia braced herself for a dressing-down to remember. "That's what I thought. Now, pack your things. You have ten minutes to meet us at the road."

"Are we leaving?"

"Nine minutes, Agnolo."

"Ser." Orelia tapped her fist against her chest in salute and hurried off down the road to the crumbling cottage where she had been quartered with an old grandmother and her widowed son. Both were still out either cleaning fish or braiding rope at the wharf. The inside smelled of herbs and salt, comforting even as it stung the nose.

Donning her armor as quickly as she could, Orelia shoved her sparse other personals into her satchel and gave the tiny bed she had called hers for the last couple of weeks a mournful look before hurrying out the door.

Only Cirino waited for her just outside the north edge of the village, where the proper king's road passed the footpath that led to Tamini.

"They went ahead," he said, tossing her the reins of her horse.

She caught them and climbed into the saddle, nudging the horse forward after the other knight. "Where?"

"Ahead. Remo said we should follow the road and we'll find them."

It was a long and quiet ride. Cirino wasn't one for idle conversation, but at least he didn't ridicule her like the rest of their company. The hours crawled as Orelia fought to keep her drooping eyes open, and the few breaks they took were short. When they finally caught up to the others, they already had camp set up and a fire going.

"You finally made it," Leon hollered as soon as he spotted Orelia and Cirino. She ignored him, instead looking at the rest of the knights spread out. Santo was missing. "Remo's got a job for you."

"Oh?" she said, trying not to let her frustration out in her exhaustion, focusing on untacking her horse.

"Over by the wagon. Word to the wise, keep your fingers out of the bars."

Bars?

Orelia leaned around her horse, squinting at the wagon. Sure enough, the back had been converted from the canvas covering that had carried and protected their supplies to something more like an iron cage with wheels. Inside, she could make out the shadowy outline of a figure sitting hunched within, but it was too far out of the firelight for her to make out much else.

Had they picked up a prisoner in need of transport? When had all of this happened?

Hobbling her horse, she hefted her tack and set it with the rest piled at the base of a massive oak. All the while, she felt the men watching her, their eyes tracking her like wolves as she crossed the camp.

Remo was waiting around the other side of the wagon, his eyes glinting in the firelight. He gestured to the cage. "Make yourself useful and keep an eye on this beast. And while you're here, get it to eat."

"I… Yes, ser," she said uncertainly, peering into the cage, but backlit as it was by the fire, she still couldn't make out much other than a vague shape. "What a—"

Remo kicked a bucket by her foot, sending up a waft of buzzing flies and the foul scent of offal that made her eyes water. "Hurry up. You're on first shift."

Orelia cut her eyes at him before she could stop herself, quickly shifting them past to the dark wood crowding around them. "Yes, ser," she said, keeping her voice as even as possible.

His gaze bore into her as he walked past. She waited until the crunch of his boots faded before letting out a tight sigh and looking at the cage. She could faintly make out the straw poking out the sides, along with strips of shredded leather and torn rope.

"How're you supposed to eat this?" she murmured, wrinkling her nose as she bent to pick up the disgusting bucket, hefting it up to the edge of the wagon. "I know it's disgusting, but maybe we can pretend—"

She saw the eyes first, a flickering glow like a creature in the woods that disappeared as quickly as they appeared. She froze, squinting into the cage where she could just make out the outline of shoulders and a head as the prisoner shifted, the firelight catching their features. Soft, round, brown cheeks streaked with tears and delicately plump lips that were twisted down into an angry scowl, and for a moment, Orelia thought they had captured a woman, until she made out the rest of her.

It wasn't hair framing her face, but feathers, and what Orelia had thought were rags were yet more feathers clothing her, black as the night.

"A harpy," Orelia breathed. "Commander?"

Remo hadn't gone far yet, but the only inclination he had heard her was how his chin lifted while he continued to go through their supplies, passing rations to Cirino, who passed them out amongst the others.

"What are we doing with a harpy, ser?"

"You're familiar with the Boni menagerie, no?" Remo said flatly. "I trust you can figure it out."

She set her teeth at the name, letting the anger it inspired pass through her. "A new pet?" she quested, gingerly reaching into the bucket for what seemed like the least unappetizing piece of offal.

"Indeed. Lord Boni is paying a premium for a healthy harpy, so get it to eat."

"Yes, ser." Pinching what she thought might be a piece of liver with the tips of her fingers, Orelia drew it out and flicked it between the bars.

The harpy flinched as the offal landed near her. With a low hiss, it kicked at the grotesque meat with a flash of long, curved talons, shoving the food out between the bars again.

"Come on, now." Orelia picked another piece out, holding it just within the bars. "I know you have to be hungry," she coaxed, trying not to pay attention to her own growling stomach.

"I'm not," the harpy replied quietly.

The hunk of meat slipped from Orelia's fingers with a wet plop. "You can speak."

The harpy's head cocked very slightly. "Of course, I can." She lowered her arms to the straw-covered floor and crawled towards Orelia. When she reached the bars, the harpy grabbed them with delicate, clawed hands and leaned forward. "I don't want food. I want out. I wouldn't hurt anyone, I'd leave."

Orelia's eyes flicked low to the harpy's bare chest, sculpted perfectly like that of a woman's. Gods. "I can't..." Orelia glanced past the harpy at the fire, at the other knights watching her, and lowered her voice. "I can't let you out."

"You can, but you won't." The harpy accused quietly and sank back to sit on the floor. "You're all cruel monsters."

Said a harpy, eater of men, Orelia reminded herself. Sirens were beautiful for a reason. "Will you eat?"

"No," the harpy insisted. "Would you eat it? Sour, rotten meat from a sick pig?"

Orelia looked down at the bucket, her nose wrinkling. It was pointless to argue further. "I'll see what can be done," she assured the harpy, setting the bucket down and rounding the wagon to join the others.

The knights had been laughing about something when Orelia approached them. Several looked at her, while the others kept eating. But none of them spoke, except Remo. "Aren't you supposed to be watching the harpy?"

"The meat's off," she said, bracing for his retort.

Remo got up and paced towards her. "I've seen birds eat worse. You're supposed to get it to eat. I don't care how you do it."

"I will. I'm going to try something else."

The commander sighed impatiently as he approached, one hand idly tapping on the pommel of his sword at his waist. "Then what are you doing over here?"

She looked pointedly at the fire. "Trying something else."

Remo followed her gaze to the fire, where some of the men were heating or cooking food over it. "You are *not* feeding that thing our rations," he said firmly.

"I'll give it some of mine. If it eats, then it won't get sick before we get to Boni's estate."

"You won't be getting more than your share," Remo reminded.

"Commander—" One of the knights began to protest, but paused when Remo turned and looked at him.

Orelia squared her shoulders with a stoic nod. "That's fine."

"Go on, then." Remo waved her on, but something felt off with how easily he acquiesced to her decision. Even the most pointless things often came with an inane argument, if not from Remo, then with several of the other knights. But none of them really provided any comment, just watched her as she went to fetch her own evening meal.

She grabbed a roasted fish that had been left for her, a loaf of bread, and a mug of beer, and retreated to the harpy's cage. She held the fish out through the bars. "Try this."

The harpy looked at the offered food, eyes dilating and nose twitching before she slowly lifted an arm towards the food. She paused, watching Orelia cautiously before she took the fish. Orelia had half-expected the harpy to snatch it away, but she gently lifted it from Orelia's grasp, then retreated back to the far corner of the cage. After turning it over in her hands as though inspecting it, she used a long nail to pluck a thick flake of fish free and slipped it into her mouth.

Satisfied, Orelia kicked a clear spot on the ground, and settled down to eat. It was cold, the ground damp, but at least she could have a few moment's peace.

"Thank you," the harpy's voice came softly from the cage. She sounded sincere, if tired.

Orelia had barely gotten her teeth into her bread when a loud clatter startled her upright. The harpy scrambled in her cage, and on the opposite side of the wagon was Leon, dragging a club along the bars and laughing at the harpy. He continued around the wagon until he had circled to the side Orelia had taken up.

"One of us could've eaten that," he sneered. "That beast doesn't deserve our food after what it did to Santo. Gutted him like we gutted that pig. So, that's what it eats. Guts." He picked up the bucket full of flies and sour meat and threw its contents through the bars. Foul smelling meat and fluids slopped over the floor, dripping over the sides. The harpy let out a shrill screech, kicking straw and rotten meat out towards the knight, who retaliated with a sharp clang of the bucket against the bars. Then he threw the bucket down, nearly striking Orelia in the process.

"Let it be, Leon!" Orelia snapped, on her feet again.

"Or what?" Leon took a long stride towards her.

"Leon," Remo's voice made the knight pause. "Leave him alone. I told you, I'd deal with him. Go sit with the others."

The knight glowered at Orelia, and she held his gaze until he slunk away. She did not sit again, moving to set her back to a tree. She did not like the sound of whatever it was Remo had in store for her. Another dressing down for sympathizing with a monster, for undermining Remo's authority by suggesting a reasonable alternative, and any other number of things he might decide needed to be shouted at her.

Her commander rounded the cage, fury tight in his shoulders and fists. "That creature," he said slowly and pointed at the cage. "That thing sliced right through Santo's stomach. He was dead by the time we restrained it. It doesn't deserve *our* food or *our* compassion. Not from any of us, not even you. You've done nothing to help us on our hunts. So, you won't be getting your cut."

"You told me to get it to eat. I did," Orelia ground

through her teeth, despite every fibre of her screaming to keep her mouth shut.

"From the food we provided it," Remo barked back. "These beasts are not *pets* meant to be coddled. There was plenty of food for it, you just weren't resourceful enough to work with it."

"Or any of you."

His hand snapped out, striking her cheek harshly. "You're more trouble than you're worth. If it were up to me, you never would have been knighted. How anyone decided to take you in as their squire is beyond me."

"You could ask to have me removed from your conroi," Orelia suggested against her better judgment, swallowing the taste of blood.

"Or I could remove you myself."

His hand crossed his hip, and the hairs on the back of Orelia's neck stood on end. He'd threatened her before, but always when he was drunk, never sober, never in front of the other knights. "You'd send me back to Tamini?" she asked, hoping to guide him back to reason.

"Something far more convenient." In a blink, he shoved her into the tree at her back, pinning her with one hand, his other reaching for his side.

She moved without thinking, ramming her knee between his legs. Remo let out a shout of pain, but rather than let go, he yanked his knife free from his waist and swiped at her, the sharp edge of a dagger skimming just past her belly as she shoved him back.

His next slash barely missed her throat.

Planting her boots, she twisted out of the way of the next slash then drove the pommel of her sword into the man's gut. He staggered, wheezing, but his gaze never left her, searing into her with such visceral hate. He was going to kill her.

"What do you think you're doing?" she shouted, finally freeing her blade in time to meet his as he lunged again. Their swords met in a deafening clash she could feel vibrate all the way down both arms.

"What someone should have done a long time ago," he spat.

There was movement behind him, and Orelia flicked a glance past to see the other knights forming around them, their swords drawn. They…

With a snarl, Remo knocked her sword away and swung again.

A line of fire opened along her arm, and Orelia clenched her teeth around a scream, keeping her sword up as another bone shaking blow connected with her blade. She had to get away. She had to run before the others closed off her escape. She—

An arm snapped around her neck from behind, dragging her off balance before pain, sharp and biting and hot seared across Orelia's back, peeling a scream from her. She clawed at the man's arm, his face, anything she could reach.

"Do it now!" Leon shouted at her ear.

"No! No!" Orelia screamed, kicking at Remo. This couldn't happen. Not like this. She had to get away. Had to find someone, anyone.

Steel cut into bone as Remo slashed at her legs, but she kept kicking anyway. Kept fighting, even as the grip at her neck tightened, strangling her screams, and the firelight began to dim in front of her eyes. She could only watch as Remo lunged past her kick, the tip of his sword plunging into her belly, stealing her screams away in a last, horrid gasp.

Everything seemed to go still in that moment, their figures frozen as if the gods had turned them into terribly real statues, caught forever in their tableau.

Orelia lowered her eyes, staring at the place the sword disappeared into her, at the red stain slowly blooming across her blue gambeson, her lips moving in a single word. "Oh."

With a wrench, Remo tore the sword from her belly, teeth bared in a wild grin. She gasped, staggering as the grip around her neck vanished, her fingers clutching her warm, wet middle.

A boot connected with her back, knocking her to her knees. She caught herself with her sword, raising it just in time to knock Remo's second stab aside.

"Stupid bastard," Remo sneered, backhanding Orelia across the face, sparking stars across her vision.

A hand wrapped in her hair, yanking, and she staggered to her feet, swinging blindly. Her sword struck something, and she was thrown, her head striking the bars of the cage as she fell against the hard edge.

"No," she tried to scream, but it came out a harsh

wheeze. "No, you're not—Get away!" She tried to run, to crawl, to get away. She had to go. She had to find someone. She needed a doctor. She needed help. But her limbs were heavy, clumsy and slow, and all she could do was weakly cling to the cage.

There was laughter behind her before a hand closed on the back of her neck. They shoved her against the bars, their knee pressing into her back. There was a glimmer of steel, and she grabbed blindly for it, flaying her fingers along the edge of a knife as she gripped it with every ounce of strength she could muster.

"Aggie?"

That voice.

Orelia struggled to focus her gaze, expecting to find a ghost, but instead, met the harpy's golden gaze from where it cowered across the cage. It looked down at her with an expression of horror and terror behind a mask of tears, but even then, Orelia found with a new and dawning horror that she knew the face it wore, would know it anywhere amongst a thousand others.

Orelia stretched her arm through the cage, a silent plea on her lips for help, but the harpy did not move.

Shoving his knee into her back, the knight holding her ripped the blade out of her grasp and plunged the blade into her ribs.

Orelia's mouth opened, but all that came out was a long, breathless scream.

"Finally," Remo sighed at her ear, twisting the blade one last time before he wrenched it free.

She slumped against the cage, mouth opening and

closing as she tried to breathe, but her lungs didn't seem to be working anymore. "No," she sobbed, pleading even as she lay there, trying desperately to hold her blood inside her as it poured over her fingers and into the dirt. "Please… Giorgia…"

But there was no answer, only the darkening eclipse of the monster above her as Orelia's vision began to fade into unrecognizable shapes.

She was dying.

She whimpered, terrified, as she began to cry. It wasn't supposed to end this way.

There was a touch at her hand, and Orelia flinched, her voice hitching. But instead of a claw or teeth, she felt a warm hand take hers. Orelia had never felt anything so soft or gentle in any of the years since she had left her home, and for a fleeting moment, she wasn't alone in the forest, betrayed by her fellow knights. And then, with a last heavy sigh, she felt her body sink towards black oblivion, and she knew all of her struggling and fighting to prove herself had been for nothing. That this was the end of the Lady Knight of Vizeras.

Chapter Three

They'd killed him.

Xellen's breath left her as the light faded from the knight's eyes right in front of her, his body going terribly still. She hadn't wanted to believe it, even when she'd first laid eyes on those familiar golden curls and the soft angles of a face she would never forget. But then he had called her name—the one she had shed with her old life. *Giorgia.*

She couldn't believe it. She'd finally found him after so long, only to lose him again right before her eyes. She watched the men drag the body unceremoniously to the ground, torn between horror and grief.

"I told you he wouldn't put up much of a fight," the leader, Remo, laughed darkly. "Now there's nothing that will get in the way of the plan."

"What do you want us to do with him?"

Remo looked down over the body dispassionately before his eyes flicked up to Xellen, an ugly smile curling the corner of his mouth. "Strip his armor and shove him in the cage. He wanted to feed it so badly, it seems a shame not to indulge him."

There was a round of chuckling and murmured remarks before they descended on the fallen knight like vultures, pulling and yanking at the straps and ties to the armor. A few even pawed through his clothes, searching for coin or keepsakes, which they pocketed. Only one knight did not act with the others, hovering uneasily at the edge of the flock, his face pale in the orange firelight.

Once the fallen knight was bare of everything but his bloodstained clothes, two men worked to get him off the ground while a third came to the door of the cage, fumbling with a key. Xellen's feathers bristled nervously. This might be her last chance.

The moment she heard the click of the lock opening, Xellen launched herself, bracing for the pain as she rammed the metal door, nearly toppling the man. He grabbed the bars, shoving the cage door shut with an ugly curse as blood jetted down his face from his nose.

"Son of a—"

"On your right!" Remo stepped forward, sword a flash of steel as he thrust it into the cage, opening a bloody line along Xellen's scaly foot.

With a cry, she fell back, ducking another thrust as she scrambled to the opposite side where he could not reach her.

"Hurry up," he growled, slashing at Xellen again, just narrowly missing her wing.

The door opened, and the knights quickly shoved the body into the cage and slammed the door shut again, the lock clicking into place.

"There," Remo said, looking pleased as he surveyed the scene before him. "A dinner you're probably much more accustomed to, eh?"

Xellen glared at him, feathers standing on end with her fury.

"Toni, you are on first watch," Remo said, sheathing his sword as he made his way back to the fire, the others trailing after him. It was over. Xellen had missed her only chance.

Running her fingers soothingly over her wings, she finally looked down at the body sharing her prison. Slowly, she reached for the young man, rolling him onto his back and pulling him toward the center of the wagon to unfold his awkward limbs. The color and warmth hadn't even left his delicate face yet.

The murder had been such a senseless act. Agnolo didn't deserve what had happened.

"I'm sorry," Xellen said quietly, fighting tears as she traced the tips of her nails along the young man's forehead, pushing the wispy, blonde hair away and gently closing his eyelids.

For years, Xellen had wished to seek out the one person who had made her young life bearable, but she had changed, and she knew he would scarcely recognize her, let alone still want her. She should have acted sooner. She should have found a way to let him know what had happened to her. She should have done something—anything—before this. Before Agnolo…

With a deafening shriek, she threw herself against the bars, kicking and clawing and biting, but the cage wouldn't give, and knights only laughed.

"It'll tire out," Remo said, watching her with a cold dispassion that chilled her to her very core. "Give it a few hours, then we'll move again."

Xellen screamed at him, wedging her shoulders into the bars, but the space was too narrow, and the knight turned his back on her. A painful sob bubbled out of her and she swallowed it down, wrapping her arms around her legs and burying her head against her knees. Everything spilled out of her in those wretched cries. All the fear, panic, and despair.

When she ran out of energy and tears, she slid down onto her side and began to let everything slip into a numb place where she didn't have to think about anything except keeping herself tucked close and warm against the cold night.

The knights rotated watch. A few slept. Xellen couldn't bear to do the same, instead staring at the corpse sharing her cage. The color had left his face, leaving him pale and ethereal in the flickering firelight. Something twitched on his face, and Xellen sat up just enough to peer at him, certain it had been the shadows of the fire.

She reached for him, holding the back of her hand to his mouth and nose, waiting, hoping to feel even the faintest brush of breath, but there was nothing.

A trick? The last cruel joke of a dying body?

A sob worked its way into her chest, wrapping around her ribs and squeezing until she felt like she might choke, but she couldn't stop herself. Xellen slowly folded down over the body as the sobs began to build upon each other until she had her arms folded atop his still chest and lowered her head.

There was a thump beneath her palms.

Xellen slowly sat up, exhausted and puzzled. Slowly, she placed one of her hands back on Xellen's still chest, pressing down against the blood soaked cloth and feeling where his heart would be. There was another, stronger thump.

It couldn't be. He was… He had died. But as she held her hand there, she could feel the phantom pulse as it thudded dully against her hand.

Then, without any warning, the knight's body shot into a rigid bow, his ribs hitching and his mouth straining open as if trying to breathe underwater. Xellen stumbled backward in surprise, her hand lifting to cover her mouth and smother a yelp as the knight finally sucked in a ragged gasp and collapsed back to the ground, chest heaving as if he'd run a hard mile.

"Aggie?" she whispered, but there was no response. Slowly, Xellen leaned forward, giving his shoulder a firm shake. "Agnolo? Can—can you hear me?"

She cupped his face, gently turning it to her. The skin was clammy and still deathly pale, but there a faint warmth kindled under her palm. His eyes fluttered open, his gaze unfocused, and she caught a glimpse of the soft, sea-blue she'd remembered so well. Then the color seemed to change, drinking in the firelight until they were the bright, autumnal orange of the tulip trees when the seasons changed.

Just as quickly as they had opened, they slipped shut and the knight fell limp against the ground, breathing shallow, hard breaths.

He was turning. The matrons would never believe it. Aggie had always said his soul didn't match his body, and the goddess had seen. She would be reborn a harpy, just like Xellen.

Xellen picked her head up at the sound of swords being drawn and spotted the knight on duty and Remo coming closer. Crawling over Aggie, she crouched over his body, shielding him from sight with her wings and let out a sharp, short screech at the men as they approached.

"Shut up," Remo barked, stopping at the corner of the cage. "Stupid animal."

She glared at him and shifted to cover Agnolo's face from view, but the knight beneath her let out a soft, pained groan.

Remo's face contorted, the blunt irritation warping into fury. "Gods bless, he is alive."

"I know what I heard," the other knight insisted. "What do we do?"

"He won't live long the way he is."

They didn't know. Xellen wasn't sure if that was good or not. They peered through the bars for a bit longer until Remo waved a hand dismissively.

"Don't worry about it. If the harpy doesn't eat him, we'll just toss the body before we get to the Boni estate."

When they finally left, Xellen lowered herself next to Aggie, tucking as closely against the knight's side as she could to hide her tears. "Uaris protect us."

Chapter Four

The hours crawled by as the wagon rattled along the forest road, further and further from the coast. Further from Xellen's family, her flock. Further from any chance of help. Aggie twitched and whimpered in her feverish sleep, red welts rising all along her skin.

It was difficult to see her old friend in such a frightful state, but she couldn't help but feel hopeful. Growing up, *Agnolo* had never really liked his name, and had been fond of Xellen's nickname for him, *Aggie*, because it sounded like a girl's nickname. But it seemed now that he had fully adopted the identity of a woman he had always talked about wishing he could be, and the goddess Uaris had recognized his soul. Xellen was happy for him—or *her*, as she supposed was correct now, but she wished she could have been there when Orelia had finally decided to embrace her identity.

She wondered when it had happened, and what else she had missed the years they had been apart, like how her childhood best friend had become knighted. Aggie had always spoken of the idea of joining any sort of service to their lord with disdain, yet here she was, carrying a sword and dressed in a surcoat stitched with her lord's coat of arms. She wondered if it was her own death that had driven Aggie to it and, somehow, right back to her.

"What happened to you, Aggie," Xellen whispered, tracing the familiar lines of Aggie's face with the tip of one clawed finger. "Why did you come here?"

Shifting next to her, Xellen tried to make the knight as comfortable as she could. She remembered the terror and pain of her own change well. How she had felt like she was dying all over again. But every second of suffering had been worth it to be granted her wings and her flock.

Mercifully, the knights seemed to have grown bored of trying to rile Xellen up by taunting her with more rotten food and making lewd remarks about her body. A few tried to touch her when they thought she was asleep. They were lucky to keep their fingers. For now, they seemed content to chat amongst themselves about what they were going to spend their money on. It never strayed far from women.

"Another hour before we stop for camp," Remo called from his post near the front of the wagon. "We'll be on the road by dawn. We should make it to the estate in time for supper."

A chorus of cheers went up. Xellen tried to console herself that by then, she'd at least be out of the wagon.

But what then? Another cage? She couldn't survive being locked in another room, staring at the same four walls day after day. She would go mad. Again.

A soft moan interrupted the anxious spiral of her thoughts, and as she looked down into her arms again, she was met by a pair of bright orange eyes.

"Evening," Xellen whispered, praying her friend even remembered her.

The knight's brow creased, puzzled. "Giorgia?" Her voice rasped, cracked and dry, but Xellen had to bite her lip all the same to keep from weeping.

"Yes. Yes, it's me."

"What…?" Her voice broke, and she swallowed thickly, and her eyes flicked past the harpy, taking in their surroundings. Xellen wondered what the knight remembered of how she came to be in her cage. She hoped it was little, but knew better than to hold that hope too closely. "What's happening?"

"You're…changing, Aggie."

A flash of heat, of fury, lit through the knight's expression. "Orelia."

Xellen blinked, trying to decipher the word before she belatedly realized it was a name. "Orelia," she said gently.

The knight smiled faintly. "Yes."

"Orelia," she repeated again. "It's beautiful. I'm Xellen, now," she said after another pause, hoping her friend would understand.

"Xellen," the knight repeated, her head falling back, eyes slipping closed for a long moment before she looked up again. "What a dream."

Smiling, Xellen curled her wing around Orelia's face, shielding her from the knights as they began to realize she was talking to someone. "What did you dream?"

"Uaris dug me out of the sand and kissed my eyes." The knight's face flushed, her gaze going unfocused.

"The west wind?" Xellen cocked her head, amused at the confession and a little concerned for the dazed look on Orelia's face. The harpy reached out to press the back of her hand against the knight's forehead. She was burning up. "What did she look like?"

"A face gold as olive wood and hair like the night. She said 'welcome, daughter.'" Orelia smiled dreamily, cheeks flushing.

"She sounds lovely. Maybe—" A shadow passed over them and Xellen spun around to find Remo peering through the bars. Xellen bared her teeth at him, but he wasn't looking at her. He was watching Orelia.

"Still alive," he sneered, rapping the bars with his knuckles.

Xellen moved to shield the knight from his view, but by the way his eyes shot up, he had seen the changes coming about.

"You. Harpy. You can speak. I heard you. Tell me why that bastard is alive and has feathers growing out of his face."

She lifted her chin defiantly and pressed her lips together into a sneer, her feathers standing on end. "She is a harpy."

"You don't say?" He leaned forward, peering

through the bars down at Orelia. "I'll inform his lordship when we arrive that we seem to have acquired two new beasts for him."

Xellen let out a screech, and with a sharp whinny, Remo's horse skittered sideways. He snatched up the reins, bringing the horse back to heel, and glared at Xellen. "Stupid bitch." She hissed again and he nudged his horse, leading it back to its place at the front of the wagon, and leaving them in relative peace.

Xellen glared at his back, settling next to Orelia again, habitually stroking her feathers to help them lay flat again. A lord's *pet*. As if she were some common domesticated beast.

With nothing left to do but wait, Xellen laid her head on Orelia's shoulder and watched as the knight dreamt. She desperately wanted to wake her, to tell her she was sorry—sorry she had taken wing and never looked back. Sorry she had died. Sorry she had left Orelia to face a world that had betrayed them both by herself. But also how glad she was that she wasn't alone. That she finally might have a chance to tell Orelia what she couldn't bring herself to say all those years ago.

Chapter Five

Orelia drifted contentedly under the honey-sweetness of her fevered dreams. Someone was gently holding her, humming a familiar tune as they stroked her hair. The touch was warm and soft. She sighed comfortably, the scent of her comforter wild with sea spray, and Orelia was suddenly years younger, lying on the shores of a lake in the sun

She cracked her eyes, smiling as a soft, round face of sun-kissed skin came into view, framed by dark curls and crowned in sunlight above her. "We can go tomorrow," she promised that sweet face, wishing she could draw the girl down into a kiss. "Say you'll come with me."

A cloud passed over the sun, and the girl's smile faded. "I…"

"Please." The sky darkened above them, the tops of the cypress dancing as a storm began to gather.

The girl began to cry, and the surface of the lake whipped into a froth behind her. "I…"

"Please!" Orelia reached for the girl, ready to beg her, ready to tell her what would happen when she refused and went home that evening. "You can't—"

"Orelia, wake up. Wake up, it's all right."

Orelia's eyes snapped open, and she choked down a gulp of air as she surfaced from the dream into a nightmare. She was on fire, every inch of her itching as if she were being eaten alive by ants. "Oh gods," she cried, whimpering as her nails brushed a raw patch of skin.

"It's all right. I've got you."

"Who…?" Orelia's bleary gaze met the harpy's bright yellow eyes, and her heart lurched up into her throat. "No!" She flung her arm up to shield herself before the harpy could attack her, waiting for its claws to bite into her flesh.

It flinched, hopping back, and Orelia scrambled to put more space between them, her back striking metal bars. Panic began to creep in as she searched her cage for her sword, or anything that might have a sharp edge, but there was only the bloody straw, the iron cage, and the harpy squatted across from her with nothing between them.

She tried to be still, to take deep breaths and think, to remember what had happened, and how she wound up wherever this was. But the harder she tried to remember, the more her head throbbed. Pieces of memories came and went disjointedly. Flashes of golden eyes, of an eagle watching her, and the clang of metal on metal. It made as much sense as any other fever dream.

She pressed the heels of her hands into her eyes, trying to ease the pounding in her head, and went stock still at the sight of her hands.

There was blood. Old, dried, and flaking off. That in itself was horrible. But beneath the blood, something was sticking out of her skin like rows of splinters or quills. She pinched one, tugging it, but it was stuck fast. Biting her lip, she tore the splinter free, flinching at the sharp pain. Blood welled, trickling down her hand, and she ignored it to examine the splinter.

It had crumbled slightly in her grip, leaving bits of what felt like an insect's carapace on her hand along with a smear of blood. And at the center, wet and still partially coiled within its outer shell, was a feather.

"No…" She grabbed another, tearing it out of her wrist, and felt the outer shell crack in her fingers. It was a feather. They were all feathers. She was *growing feathers*. "No!"

"Stop, you shouldn't—" The harpy moved towards her without warning, reaching for her.

Orelia snatched her hand away, pressing against the bars, but there was nowhere to go, nowhere to get away. She touched her hip, then her calf, but there was neither sword nor knife, only stiff, filthy fabric.

"It's okay," the harpy said and slid back a step, her hands lifted placatingly. "It's okay."

"Why…Why am I…" Her hands went still as they passed over her middle again, sending up a waft of copper tinted air. Blood.

She pressed her fingers into her belly, expecting warmth and wetness, but there was only stiff fabric and a ragged hole. An image flickered behind her eyelids of Remo's sword sinking into her belly, of scrabbling in the dirt while her blood poured over her hands. She had been stabbed. She had been dying. But the wound was…missing.

She pulled the stained fabric apart, running her fingers over the pink, scar puckered skin. "I… I…"

"You're going to be all right, Orelia."

The knight's head shot up at her name, meeting the harpy's golden gaze. "How did you…"

"You told me," it said softly, its voice a cruel mimic of the one Orelia knew so well. "When did you change it?"

"Years ago. Why does that matter?"

"You never did like your name very much. I remember we—" The harpy's voice quivered with a small sniff, as if she were trying not to cry. "—we came up with all sorts of little nicknames, but we never used them in company. What made you finally change it?"

It sounded so much like her Giorgia, and the pain it ignited in Orelia brought with it a fury that a monster would try to imitate her friend she didn't even get to bury. "Stop," she commanded, her lips pulling back from her teeth. "Just stop. Why am I here? Why am I not…" Orelia closed her eyes against the image of Remo's sword sinking into her belly, of scrabbling in the dirt while her blood poured over her hands. "I died."

"You… did," the harpy answered gently.

Orelia sank against the bars of her cage, her knees threatening to give out. "Then this…?" She pulled her sleeve up. Her skin was pebbled with what looked like angry, risen bee stings, and at the center of each fiery red bump was a black dot.

"May I?" the harpy asked, reaching for Orelia's hand. "I've never seen that much swelling."

"What do you mean?" Orelia demanded, holding her arm out. "What's happening?"

The harpy's golden eyes flicked up at her briefly before she took Orelia's arm in both hands. Her touch was soft and cool against Orelia's feverish skin. "You… you died, by that man's blade," she reminded. "I'm not certain of the process, but it's said that women slain violently, betrayed by a man, are taken in Uaris' embrace, and we are reborn… as harpies." Xellen looked down at Orelia's arm. "These are your first feathers."

"Feathers?" Orelia wasn't certain if she was going to be sick or laugh. She hadn't survived Remo after all, but then again, she had because the gods had seen past the form she'd been cursed with at birth.

The tears she had been holding back welled and ran over, streaking down her face. She'd always known, always felt it in her heart that she was a soul born in the wrong body, and now everyone else would see too. The gods had seen.

Her knees buckled, but Orelia couldn't feel them hit the floor. Couldn't feel or hear anything past the pounding in her head. "I…I'm…"

"You're going to be all right," the harpy whispered to her, sounding so much like Giorgia tending to her on her bad days. "I'm right here. You'll be all right."

But she wasn't, Orelia thought hazily as she fought the sobs clawing their way up her throat.

She was dead.

"Well, well, well."

That voice.

Orelia spun, fear and hate and grief warring in her twisting stomach as she looked at Remo's sneering face. "You…" Lips drawing back from her teeth, Orelia threw herself against the bars, clawing at the commander, but Remo was a hair out of reach. "Why, damn you?" Orelia snarled, straining to reach him.

The commander laughed. "What else was I going to do with an aberration like you?" He set his hand on the pommel of his sword and stepped forward until he was nearly in reach, but he stayed just out of her range. "I'm sure your family will be relieved to hear about the death of their queer son. I've already sent a missive along with your belongings."

The world tilted on its axis beneath Orelia. "No." The word was hardly more than a wisp of breath. She couldn't breathe. Her parents. They'd already lost a son, and now…

She gripped the bars as if they could hold the world together around her as she fractured.

A hand settled on her shoulder, so feather-light she did not feel it right away. "Don't listen to him," the harpy said gently behind her.

"Like he ever did before," Remo laughed, his smile sharpening. "You refused to follow orders."

Orelia lifted her head, setting her shoulders as she faced him. "Only if I didn't agree with them."

"They are called orders, not suggestions. That's why I knew I couldn't trust you, you impertinent little cur."

"I am a knight, not a servant."

"No. You're not," Remo chuckled, leaning back as he looked Orelia up and down with a leer that made her wish she had on more clothes. "You're a beast."

"I am—You were the one that ordered us to—"

"Remo," Leon cut in, sauntering up behind the knight commander. "He's here."

"Finally. Stand with the others and wait for my signal."

The other knight grinned broadly, saluting the commander. "Of course." He turned away, but not before getting a look at Orelia, his nose wrinkling in disgust.

"What are you planning?" Orelia demanded, but Remo simply turned his back on her to face the courtyard beyond. It was only then that she finally realized the shadows she had taken to be the forest flanking the cart were the columns and neatly planted cypress of a garden.

A pair of liveried guards appeared at the far end, the light of their torches illuminating the pale stone of the manse behind them. A man followed behind them, dressed in rich purple and yellow.

"Lord Boni," Remo greeted the man, bowing as he set his fist to his chest. "I didn't expect you to come to see the animals yourself."

"Your letter piqued my interest," the man said, stepping up to the cage. He would have been fair in his youth, his yellow hair shot through with pieces of white under his cap and his soft chin hidden by a carefully curated beard. "I'd never heard of anything like what you were describing." he remarked, a look of fascinated disgust etched across his face as he looked down on Orelia and Xellen from outside the wagon.

"One of the knights assigned to me tried to get a bit too friendly with it the other night and got himself cursed in the process. I was going to put him out of his misery then realized the opportunity it presented."

The lord snorted drily, touching his nose. "For more money."

Remo smiled ingratiatingly. "You might just have a chance to be the first ever to breed a harpy."

Orelia reeled with disgust at being referred to like farmyard stock. "Excuse me?"

"Oh, it still talks," the lord exclaimed, leaning forward to squint through the bars.

"I'm not an '*it*'," she sneered. "I am a knight, and I was—"

"*Was* a knight," Remo echoed. "And no longer are."

"We are not cattle to be bred and sold," Xellen hissed, throwing herself against the bars with a shriek. The lord staggered back with an ugly gasp, his guards leaping to his defense, spears raised, and Orelia pulled the harpy back.

"It's perfectly safe," Remo assured Boni, cutting a dry look at the harpy.

"Very spirited!" the noble stammered, dabbing at his face with a bit of cloth. "Yes, I think I do like the idea of keeping a pair. I can offer you half the price for the male."

"She's not—"

"I'd rather think the male might be worth more than the female," Remo cut Xellen off, gesturing to the cage. "You know, not one has ever been spotted. He could be quite rare."

He. Male. *It.* Orelia could feel herself shrinking on the inside with every incorrect word. She was nothing to them. She had never been anything to them. Remo had killed her because it meant nothing.

"And you're sure it isn't some fool with an eye condition you've glued feathers on?"

"You have my word."

"I have your eagerness for my money," the lord corrected, and a flash of irritation passed over Remo's face like a shadow. "I will pay you half for the male, and if he matures as he should and produces an offspring, I will pay you another sum. That is the best I am willing to do."

"Very well," Remo said as he shifted on his feet. One hand slid behind his back, his fingers moving over something, and he extended his other hand to shake on the deal.

"I will have Franco write you up a bill and your

payment," Lord Boni said amiably, clasping Remo's hand.

Remo grinned wickedly as he yanked the noble forward, and, with a flash of steel, buried a dagger in the man's stomach. Lord Boni stared, his eyes wide, mouth agape.

A scream of anger and anguish tore its way out of Orelia, her hands flying to the scar at her middle as she watched Remo turn the dagger and plunge upwards, into the noble's ribs. Remo pulled the dagger back, but it took a second yank to free it. Lord Boni let out a pained groan and reached to clutch at Remo. The commander grabbed the noble by the jaw and lifted his knife, cutting a clean line across his throat before he shoved him down to the ground.

There were other cries and clashing of weapons, and Orelia watched in horror as the other knights fought and cut down the guards Boni had brought with him, felling them one by one.

"Gods, what is wrong with you?" she shouted, grabbing the bars and squeezing until her knuckles creaked, the smell of offal thick in her nose. "Why are you doing this?"

"For my country," he said with a cold ease that made her hair stand on end.

"What does that mean? How are you—You killed him! You all killed all of them."

Remo snickered, bending to wipe his blade off on the grass. "Only the people who would have gotten in our way."

"Of what?"

"You don't need to know, beast."

All of the knights under Remo's command seemed largely unbothered by the murders they had committed. Two of them reached for the nearest body and lifted it between them to carry away. This had all been planned.

"Get the wagon inside," Remo barked. "Put these creatures into their new enclosure. And find the *new* Lord Boni for me."

Chapter Six

The Boni estate's menagerie was renowned throughout Castanneos and even beyond. Xellen had heard stories of it growing up—of the exotic and sometimes mythical creatures kept within for anyone to come and see for themselves. The idea had enchanted her as a girl. A place to see all the wonders of the world. But now, as the wagon carrying her rolled through the towering gates and into the sprawling stone building that was to be her prison, she could only feel horror and dismay to see the rows and rows of animals locked behind iron bars.

Countless pairs of pitiful eyes watched them pass, creatures she didn't even have names for, until they came to an empty cage. It had been decorated with the hollow remnant of a long dead tree, its grey wood smooth of bark, and a shallow pool of water. Plants in earthen pots crowded the corners, and at the center of the cage, a crude wooden box on stilts with a ramp leading up into it provided some sort of shelter, if not privacy.

Using a hidden mechanism, one of the guards escorting them caused a panel of the bars to lift away while the other guards unhitched the horse and led it to a post nearby. Setting their shoulders to the wagon, all three strained to push it into place at the opening before setting the brake.

"Ready?" one of them asked, and they all moved to take positions around the wagon.

A thrill of panic lit through Xellen. This was it. If they didn't escape now, she and Orelia were going to be locked away for good. She crowded towards the back of the cage, searching desperately over every inch of the cage for some way out.

Orelia, however, sat in the center of the wagon, unmoving, her head hung low as the guards unlatched the front of the cage on the wagon with a long hook on the end of a spear shaft, and pushed it open.

"In you go, birdies," the guard sniggered, clanging the hook on the side of the cage.

"Never!" Xellen shrieked, yanking at the bars, but they were as firm as ever.

The guards exchanged looks, and the one holding the hook gestured at the other two. "Get 'em up. I don't wanna be out here all night."

The other two smiled cruelly and took positions on opposite sides of the wagon. "Come on, birdies. In you go." Sticking their spears through the bars, they jabbed at Xellen, and not gently.

She squealed as one of the steel points caught her

wing, drawing a fiery line of blood. She grabbed the weapon, tugging at it. But when the point of the other weapon jabbed painfully into her back, she lost her grip.

"None of that, now," the guard chastised.

She glared at him, and snatched at the spear again, only to receive another hard jab. "Let us out!"

"Stop your squawking," the guard with the hook said, leaning into the haft of his tool. "If you want to sit in that cage all night, that's fine with me. My orders are to stay here until the job's done, and I've got plenty to keep my occupied right here." He leered at Xellen's chest, then reached down to adjust himself, and she clasped her wings tight to cover her breasts. "It's too bad about that curse," he continued, glancing at Orelia. "I guess I'll have to use my imagination. I'll bet it's tight enough to raise a blister."

Xellen looked between them all, hardly believing what she was hearing, but they were all looking at her like a bunch of slavering dogs.

There was a touch at her side, and she nearly jumped out of her skin, skittering sideways until she realized it was Orelia. "Stay close," the knight murmured, her tone light and comforting, but Xellen knew the look on Orelia's face well, even if she'd only seen it once that last day they'd met at the lake.

"You can wank on your own time. I'd like to get back to my supper," one of the other guards complained, sliding his spear through the bars again.

In a flash, Orelia caught the spear just behind the head, yanking it hard enough, the guard lost his grip and smacked his head into the side of the wagon with a loud clang. Surging to her feet, she wrestled with the spear to pull it in the cart, when the other guard jabbed at her from the other side, and she caught it in her other hand.

"Hey now!" the man with the hook shouted, rushing to help as Orelia smashed the butt of a spear into one of the men's heads. He grabbed hold of it, along with the guard still clinging to it, and they pulled, nearly upsetting Orelia's balance as the first guard righted himself. With a cry, he yanked the spear back and shoved it through the bars as hard as he could, plunging it into her thigh.

She collapsed to her knee with a heart-rending scream, and Xellen threw herself against the bars, her claws raking over the man's face. He staggered back, screaming as blood ran down his face and through his fingers, dragging the spear with him.

"You bitch!" the other guard roared, throwing himself against the spear.

"No!" Xellen cried, lunging across the cage as the haft slipped through Orelia's fingers.

With a momentous shout, the knight thrust the tip away, only to meet the curved hook in the side of her head and she tumbled bonelessly to the floor.

Xellen swept after the weapons, but the guards yanked them free before she could catch them, stepping well out of reach.

"Damned monsters," the guard with the hook swore, wiping his forehead.

"Why?" Xellen shouted, straining to reach them,

furious tears streaming down her face.

"Because the lord likes pretty things to look at, even if they are just monsters." He hefted his hook, all traces of his earlier lewdness replaced entirely by a hard fury. "Now, you take that other one and go on in, or we'll finish him off. His lordship only wanted one harpy, after all."

There was a soft groan behind her, and, still shaking with anger, Xellen turned to help Orelia as she stirred. "It's all right," she murmured, touching the side of the woman's head where blood had dyed her fine golden hair a sticky red. "I've got you." She helped the knight stagger to her feet, straining to support her as Orelia leaned on her to take a limping step forward, then another.

They stopped at the end of the cage, at the threshold between prisons, and Xellen swallowed. This was it.

"Go on," goaded the guard, and, choking down her fear, Xellen carried Orelia into their new cage as the bars closed shut behind them. She was trapped again, only this time, there was no escape, no window to creep through to freedom.

Ignoring the guards as they swore and spat behind her, she set one foot and then the other on the ramp leading up to the nestbox, Orelia stumbling at her side. It was little better than a chicken coop at the top, strewn with straw, but it was softer than the stone floor. "Orelia?" she murmured, helping to ease the knight down.

She groaned, hissing as she sank into a sitting

position. "I'm all right."

"Are you sure? Your leg—"

"Only a flesh wound," she gritted through her teeth, pressing her palm into her thigh. "It'll be all right as long as it doesn't go off."

Xellen watched as the circle of red stretched and grew on Orelia's breeches. "You're sure?"

Orelia nodded, jaw tight. "Had enough of them to know."

"You—You have?" Xellen crouched next to her friend, trying to imagine what she had been through to get to this place and time. She stole a glance at the knight's face, spotting the delicate down that had started to come through. If they were with the flock, they would be doting on the new fledgling, helping her preen and providing a salve for the itching. But Orelia didn't have a flock. Just her.

"I'm sorry I couldn't… Couldn't stop them," Orelia said, her voice catching thickly as she looked down at her hands, at the cracks bleeding at her knuckles and the dots of blood on her wrists where she had plucked out her pin feathers and scratched her skin raw. "We lost our best chance at escape."

"We'll find another way," Xellen soothed.

"Perhaps, but where am I supposed to go?"

"Away from here."

"Where? I can't go home. I can't…" Orelia's eyes brimmed, her hands clenching into shaking fists. "There's nowhere I can go."

"You could come with me," Xellen offered, her face

flushing as she rushed to add, "You could stay with my flock."

Orelia's face creased with confusion. "With the harpies?"

Xellen tried to smile reassuringly, despite everything. "Yes."

"They would have me, even though I'm…?"

"A harpy?" Xellen offered her hand, an olive branch, a bridge, a comfort, whatever Orelia needed it to be. "Of course."

The knight looked at it, the first tears turning to a sob before she grasped Xellen's hand like a lifeline. The harpy pulled her friend into her embrace, rocking her gently as she squeezed her tight, her heart aching for all those missing years between them. How many times had Orelia fallen apart like this since Xellen knew her as a child? And how many times had she had to do it alone after Xellen left her behind?

"It'll be all right," she whispered, stroking the silk-fine hair as she cradled Orelia. "We'll figure something out."

Chapter Seven

Everything ached.

Orelia pressed more deeply into the warm softness along her back and side, willing herself to sleep again, but she could already feel the drum starting up inside her head.

"Ngh." Cracking one eye open, she winced at the shaft of light cutting across her vision, blurring everything into a smear of brown and white.

When she finally blinked her eyes clear, she realized she was looking at a large wing draped over her, a hand at the far end of it curled against the straw.

The harpy.

Orelia heard a noise behind her and she froze, watching the harpy's clawed finger tips curl inward. But then she felt something warm and soft against her neck and felt a breath of warm air tickle her ear.

Xellen.

Orelia sank back, rolling off her sore hip, and distinctly felt two firm mounds of breasts press against her back. Her eyes shot open, her face igniting in a scarlet blush. She—

"Orelia?" the harpy murmured almost at her ear, sending a cascade of gooseflesh down her neck and arms.

"I'm awake."

Xellen shifted behind her, her wing drawing close around Orelia. "How do you feel?"

"I'll be fine. I've pushed through worse," Orelia insisted.

"You've always been strong, but this is different."

Gods, she sounded so much like Giorgia. Orelia rolled onto her back, peering up at the harpy. She looked just like her. Soft, delicate features, the smattering of freckles, thick, dark curls that hugged her neck and shoulders. Even her soft lips. "Are you…really her? Giorgia?"

The harpy smiled, the same way Orelia remembered, and her chest ached. "Who else could I be?"

"A dream." Orelia lifted a hand to touch one of the soft curls. "A nightmare to torment me while I await judgment."

"I could never torment you." The harpy lifted her hand until her fingers brushed Orelia's wrist, her eyes— her golden eyes—crinkling in amusement. "You've been reading too much poetry again, haven't you?"

The knight groaned, winding her finger about the curl. She wanted to believe so badly what every one of her senses was screaming at her. "How did you come to be like this?"

The harpy's eyes watered and she looked away, blinking rapidly. "The same way as all the others. Same as you."

Orelia stiffened. "Someone killed you?"

"I…don't remember much. Thankfully." Her voice trailed off briefly. "Just that I woke up in the care of my flock, feverish, bandaged. Changing."

An old shame coiled in Orelia's belly. She should have been there. The letter she had gotten had said there'd been an accident, not that someone had… But her regret couldn't eclipse the sudden overwhelming joy of realizing she was looking at her friend again. Could touch and see her, real as the bars of their cage, or anything else. She was alive, and Orelia couldn't stop the first hot tears from falling down her cheeks. "I never knew what happened. All I was given was a letter from your mother."

The harpy let out a soft noise and pressed her forehead to Orelia's shoulder, sniffling softly. "I thought I'd never see you again."

"Why didn't you write, or something—anything to let me know you were alive?"

"You wouldn't have recognized me, and I-I feared you would have struck me down for how monstrous I had become."

The words were like a kick to the knight's chest. "From a letter?"

"Would you have believed a letter? How would I have even gotten it to you?" She withdrew her wing from around Orelia, swiping at her eyes. "I-I'm sorry. I was scared."

Orelia looked away, hurt and ashamed. "I suppose it doesn't matter now, anyway."

The harpy didn't say anything at first, wiping at her face. "I'm... I'm glad to see you, regardless of the circumstance," she finally said, her voice shy.

Orelia managed a nod, fighting the tears brimming in her eyes as well. "I wish—"

A sharp metal clang reverberated through the shelter, nearly starting Orelia out of her skin. Behind her, Xellen let out a sharp, distressed chirp, wings flailing. "What—"

"Come out, birds," Remo's voice drawled from outside. "There's breakfast."

Xellen's feathers bristled and she leaned to peer out the door, then looked at Orelia. "There's a new man. I don't recognize him."

Pushing up on her elbow beneath the harpy, Orelia strained until she could peer out of the entrance of the nest. Standing outside the bars was Remo and several of the other knights. And with them, dressed in velvet and gold, was a man Orelia didn't recognize either, but she could hazard a guess

The *new* Lord Boni smiled, teeth flashing white behind his carefully trimmed beard. "Ah, there are my new little pets. Come, let me look at you. I've brought breakfast."

Remo tossed a pair of hares through the bars onto the ground, bloody and limp.

"You stay here. I'll get it," Xellen said and reached

to pull Orelia back.

"Wait. They just want to ogle you."

Xellen gave her a little smile. "I know. But we need to eat. Especially you."

"Me? Wait, Xell…" But the harpy had climbed out already. She stayed crouched, her bird-like feet bent and her arms tucked close to her sides. When any of the men moved, she paused, her feathers puffing until they stilled.

"She's gorgeous," the lord said with a breathy sigh. "I've never seen one up close. I was told they were monstrous."

"Considering she gutted one of my men, I'd say she is," Remo sneered, looking over Xellen's head directly at Orelia.

"Cost of business," Lord Boni dismissed. "Imagine if they could be trained." He knelt just outside the bars, watching Xellen creep closer towards the hares, his head tilting down to look low on her. "She looks soft, doesn't she? I think she'd look lovely in some chains."

Xellen froze at that and quickly backed up.

"They can understand us," Remo said flatly. "And can speak."

"Is that so? Come on, sweetheart. We've brought you breakfast, one for each of you. Why don't you come out?" the man asked, leaning to peer into the nesting box. "Let me see you."

Orelia shrank out of view, pressing into the wall, and she heard the man scoff.

"He's shy, isn't he?"

"Embarrassed, more likely." Remo scoffed. "He did get himself cursed."

"I'm not cursed," Orelia sneered, sitting up to glare at Remo. "You killed me and then sold me."

"I can see very well you are not dead," Lord Boni remarked, his grin stretching as he turned to Remo. "Do you think he'll survive?"

"I'm certain of it," Remo said, his eyes cutting to Orelia. "Nothing else has gotten rid of him."

"Excellent. If I can get them to breed, I can only imagine what people would pay to see the first fledgling harpy."

"Happy to have pleased his lordship," Remo replied drily.

The lord looked back at Xellen as she leaned to snatch up the hares and clutched them to her chest. "I think I'd like to have a perch made for this one. For the dining hall." He watched her retreat back towards the nesting box.

"I'd recommend a strong collar and chain as well," Remo said.

"Of course, once we have the perch made. Until then, enjoy your breakfast." And with that, the group of men moved away.

All of them, except Remo. He stayed there, arms folded behind his back. He regarded Orelia with a look somewhere between marvel and disgust. "It seems you weren't entirely worthless after all, Agnolo."

"Why?" Orelia sneered. "You still haven't told me a damn reason why."

"What does it matter to you, bird? The only thing you'll have to worry about from now on is where your next hare is coming from. Why, I'm almost envious."

"Don't listen to him," Xellen said when she reached the nest box. "Come on, we need to eat."

Orelia glanced at the hares, swallowing thickly at the raw, bloody carcass. "I hope your luck gives out when you need it most," she spat at Remo, retreating into the box where she couldn't see her old knight commander wearing new livery in different colors than they had worn leaving the king's court.

Xellen let out a sharp huff as she dragged the hares into the corner. "I'm sorry it's raw," the harpy said over her shoulder while she skinned and pulled at the meat where Orelia couldn't quite see. "Usually we give the fledglings food they are more familiar with. But you won't get sick from this, I promise." She turned and held her hand out to Orelia. Nestled in the middle of her palm was a piece of raw meat. "If you have trouble with it, I would just swallow it quickly."

"Gods, I..." It was raw, still bleeding over the harpy's palm. "I don't think I'm hungry."

"I know," Xellen said softly. "But your body is changing and it's been two days at least. We aren't likely to get anything else."

Orelia swallowed. Eat raw meat or starve.

Hesitantly, she pinched the bit of meat with the tips of her fingers, holding it up. Her stomach flip flopped at the sight of it, but if she wanted to survive whatever was happening to her and confront Remo, she had to eat. She popped the meat into her mouth and, as quickly as she could, chewed a few times, trying to get it down. The texture was awful, but to her surprise, the meat didn't taste bad. In fact, it was very nearly…sweet. It was good.

"At least it's fresh," Xellen said as she tore off another piece for herself, then offered another piece to Orelia.

Mouthwatering, Orelia took the next piece, her stomach letting out an eager growl. Among every little ache and pain, at least Orelia would not have to deal with hunger. For now, anyway.

All too soon, the meat was gone, and Orelia found herself wavering where she sat, her head heavy and throbbing.

"How are you feeling?" Xellen asked, scrubbing her hands with straw.

Orelia shivered, her skin prickling. "Cold."

The harpy shifted closer, pressing the back of her hand to Orelia's forehead. "Your fever is back. You should get some rest. I can keep you warm."

"I've heard that before."

Xellen tilted her head, then giggled as her cheeks heated. "I didn't mean it like that."

"Shame," Orelia mumbled, letting herself enjoy the way Xellen's blush darkened.

The harpy scooted into the corner of the box and held a hand out to beckon her. Haltingly, Orelia crawled over, letting Xellen guide her down until she was curled on her side under Xellen's wing. She was much taller than Xellen, but the harpy did her best to press against her, covering as much of her exposed, shivering body as she could.

"Is this all right?" Xellen murmured.

Orelia could hardly keep her eyes open. "Mmhm."

"Good." Xellen nestled closer, and Orelia soaked in the warmth and the feeling of another person against her. Gods, had it really been five years since she'd willingly lain with someone? It felt so much longer. But then, in her dreams, it always seemed like just yesterday.

Rolling back into the embrace, she let herself drift into the warmth of her reveries. They were all she had left of her life, after all.

Chapter Eight

Xellen had always been an early riser, enjoying the quiet peace that seemed to befall the world in the hours before the sun rose. It had been the only time in her family's house she felt truly content—seated at her window as she watched the horizon tint pink and listened to the birds as they stirred. It was one of those early mornings that she had first met her neighbor chasing an escaped puppy under her window and cursing like a sailor. She could still remember that morning so clearly. The awkward, gangly youth smeared in mud and scratched to ribbons. Their golden hair falling from its neat queue.

Leaning out her casement, Xellen had offered a bit of stale pastie to lure the pup out of the bramble rose it had taken shelter beneath. In return, Orelia had plucked one of the roses from the vine and handed it to her. The flower had barely opened, just showing its dusty pink petals, but the perfume of it filled her room with the sweetest scent as she watched her neighbor wrestle the puppy under one arm with an even number of curses and sweet praises for the squirming creature.

They'd each lifted a hand in parting, and Xellen watched as this new stranger hurried back across the lawn as the sun crept higher and servants began to stir. Little did she know she would come face to face with the same golden haired youth later that day, when her family received some unexpected guests who'd come to learn what new neighbors had taken the country home next to theirs.

Everything had been so simple during those summers. If only they could have lasted.

Tendering a sigh, Xellen quietly nestled closer to Orelia. A small mess of hair had fallen over the knight's face in her sleep, and Xellen traced her finger under the hair, tucking it behind her friend's ear so she could see the fledgling's lovely face. She looked relaxed for the first time since they met, her hands tucked beneath her chin, knees drawn up together. It reminded Xellen distantly of a cat curled up in the sun.

She traced another finger along the rigid new feathers of Orelia's arm. More had come in while they slept, but they were still enclosed in tiny stiff shafts that needed preening. Without thinking, Xellen pinched one of the pins, breaking the shaft and freeing the feather, only for the knight to suddenly twitch awake.

"Sorry," Xellen whispered, retracting her hand.

"Hm?" Twisting in Xellen's arms, Orelia blinked blearily up at the harpy, an absent smile crossing her lips. Xellen couldn't help but smile and duck her head, surprised by the heat filling her cheeks.

"Good morning," she greeted. "Sorry if I woke you."

"What were you doing?" Orelia mumbled sleepily, her head nestling against Xellen's chest.

"Just trying to help," Xellen said, brushing her fingers over another stiff pin feather. "You'll feel better once these are all preened."

Lifting one of her arms, Orelia turned it over, examining the golden brown feathers next to the dark, quill-like sheaths. "How did you get them to do that?"

"Here, I'll show you." Xellen held her hand out, patiently waiting until Orelia set her arm in the harpy's palm. "You just pinch it like this, see? And you give it a little twist." She did so, the sheath flaking under her fingertips. She pulled it away and then smoothed the feather. "They're a pain to do yourself, but they shouldn't bother you as much once they're free."

Orelia hummed softly in reply, pinching the next feather and peeling the sheath away, fingers twitching. "It tickles."

"Does it?" Xellen grinned. "I don't remember if mine tickled when I changed. The first couple of days were a bit of a blur. But they do drive me crazy while I'm molting."

"Anything is better than that itch. Gods, I thought I'd go mad from it alone."

"I'm sorry you had to put up with it. And… all of this, really." Xellen hesitantly reached to help preen Orelia's arm. "I wish I could have done something."

"There's nothing you could have done. I don't think anyone could have helped me."

"I know." But that didn't stop her from remembering the knight's face as she died right in front of her. "But at least… at least I can help you here. Help you survive and adjust… escape, eventually." Xellen brushed the pile of feather shafts from Orelia's arm. "For what it's worth, I'm glad I'm not alone."

Orelia sighed, her mouth tightening in a grimace. "Me too."

"If we…" Xellen swallowed, picking at another pin feather to distract her from her sudden nerves as she tried to get her tongue to form the words she wanted to ask—ones that sounded far too like the ones she had turned away five years ago. "*When* we get out of here you could… come with me," Xellen offered haltingly.

Orelia tilted her head, studying Xellen, and the harpy's face flushed darkly. "With the other harpies?"

"It—It's safer in flocks," Xellen stammered, fixing her gaze on the feather she was preening. "We look after each other."

The knight was quiet, lips pressing in thought. "I don't think I'd be welcome," she said after a moment.

"Why do you think that?"

Orelia gave her an arch look. "I'm not blind to what I look like to other people. I've heard it my whole life."

"You're a harpy now," Xellen said confidently, squeezing Orelia in her embrace. "It doesn't matter what you looked like before."

The knight's eyes glistened, fixing on the roof.

"You're sure?"

Xellen lowered her head, pressing a silent kiss into Orelia's soft hair. "Of course."

"What about Remo, though?"

"What about him?"

Orelia's hand came up to hers, stroking her feathers soothingly. "I know he's planning more than helping some ambitious lordling take over his relative's estate."

"Then someone will stop him. It's none of our concern now. The only thing we need to concern ourselves with is finding a way out and finding a flock."

"I'll get us out. But I have to stop Remo."

"But why risk it?"

"It is what a knight does. I have a duty to uphold."

Xellen cupped Orelia's cheek, wiping away the first trickle of tears. "You don't owe duty to those who killed you."

"Not to them. To the people they might hurt." She raised her chin, finally looking at Xellen again, tearfully determined. "They were willing to kill a noble of one of the great houses in cold blood. They are planning something, and I can't let them get away with it, not when I can do something."

"But you're—" She wasn't a knight anymore, but Xellen didn't know how to make the fledgling understand. And when she looked at Orelia, at the determination in her face, she couldn't bring herself to try and dissuade her. "All right. We'll think of something. But you have to focus on keeping your strength up for now."

Orelia sighed, seeming to relax at that. "You're right. How long will this take?"

"Normally a few days. The down comes in first and fast, but the larger feathers take longer. Your claws and teeth will come in after that. Then, you can learn to fly."

"To fly." The knight chuckled wistfully. "I don't feel like I could even manage walking at the moment. My feet…" She shifted uncomfortably, wincing.

Xellen darted a glance down at Orelia's feet, but of course, her boots were still on. If her feet had started to change, though, there was no room for them to grow. Sitting up, she started to reach for them, then checked herself. She and Orelia weren't that close anymore. "May I see?"

A faint color rose high in Orelia's cheeks. "Fine," she relented, not quite looking at Xellen.

The harpy smiled and eased into a crouch. Grasping the heel of Orelia's boot, she had to pry it loose, teeth set to her lip, until it finally came free. Even in her hose, it was plain to see Orelia's foot had changed. The toes were longer, curling in towards the arch of her foot, which seemed to have lengthened. The nails had fallen away, collecting in the bottom of her boot, leaving the tips of her toes bloody and raw.

"Oh, goddess," Xellen whispered. "They're farther along than I expected."

Orelia glanced at Xellen's feet—large, scaled, and taloned like an eagle's—and her face paled. "They're cold," she complained, flexing her foot, the muscles trembling.

"You should get the hose off, too," Xellen said, tugging gently at Orelia's other boot. Orelia shot her a look, and Xellen realized exactly what her suggestion might have sounded like. "Y-You'll feel better. You can stretch your toes out and-and it won't irritate your feathers."

The second boot came free, and Orelia whimpered in relief. Her other foot was just as bad as the first one, maybe even more curled and seized up.

"I can step out if it will make you more comfortable," Xellen offered.

Orelia seemed to hesitate. "It's…all right," she finally said, reaching beneath her filthy gambeson and plucking at something. Then, hooking her thumbs in the top of one hose, she slid it free.

Xellen started to look away when she caught a glimpse of pale thighs, but she noticed the small bulge of undergarments before Orelia tugged her shirt down. Some down had come through on her legs, but the rest of the feathers were still coming in, peppering her angry, red skin with black, needle-like protrusions. Hopefully, it would settle soon.

Taking a look at Orelia's feet, she was relieved to see the talons already growing in where the nails had fallen. Despite the blood, they were in better shape than she had expected. "You can press your foot on the wall, if you want to stretch it out. Or, I-I could help."

"I'd rather not," Orelia said, untying her other hose and peeling it off with a shiver, her eyes slanted away from the sight of her own legs.

"I promise to be gentle. And you said they were cold."

Orelia shifted uncomfortably, tucking her legs close. "I—"

A light *clang* made Xellen jump and she peered out of the nesting box. It wasn't Remo or some other sneering guard, but one of the knights, leaning to look through the bars in their direction before he gently tapped his gauntlet against the bar again. "I came to speak with Agnolo," he called, peering up into the nest box.

Xellen's feathers bristled along her neck and shoulders. "There's no Agnolo here."

"I can see him—"

"You're mistaken," Xellen cut him off, stalking down the box's ramp, wings flared to block his view of Orelia. "There is no Agnolo here."

"But he's—"

"She," Orelia finally corrected from behind Xellen.

The knight swallowed, his expression contorting in confusion. "She," he repeated carefully. "Look, I just want to talk to you," he said over Xellen's head.

The wood creaked behind her, and Xellen whirled as Orelia crawled into the entrance of the box. "Wait—"

"I want to hear what he has to say," Orelia croaked, pulling herself to her feet using the frame of the entrance. Her toes remained curled in, the muscles trembling, and Xellen hurried to offer her hand.

"Let me help you."

Orelia clasped the harpy's hand, and Xellen tried not to stare at the dark bruising under her nail beds. She was going to lose those nails soon too. Her change was accelerating.

She took a cautious step forward away from the support of the wall, high stepping around the awkward shape of her changing feet. The other knight watched them, his eyes wide in awe and horror in equal measure. Clinging to Xellen's hand, Orelia made it to the bottom of the ramp, and looked the other knight in the eyes, her jaw tight with closely reined fury. "I'm listening, Cirino."

"You…" He glanced around suddenly, as if expecting someone to jump from the shadows. "You really are changing." He wiped a bead of sweat from his forehead, his face sickly pale. "I swear… I swear I didn't know Remo would go this far. I would have warned you if I knew."

"What do you mean '*this far*'? You knew he was planning something?"

The knight shifted uneasily, looking around him again, anywhere but at Orelia. "He talks when he gets drunk. Talks about all these plans, and says…says *things* he'd like to do, but I thought it was just talk."

"He talked about me?"

Cirino nodded weakly.

Xellen's gut twisted inside of her. She had never, in her experience, caught a man saying anything savory about a woman behind closed doors.

"What else?" Orelia demanded. "Did he mention—

"

"I don't know. It was nonsense. Glory and revolution. He's always been one of those that hated the royal family."

"If you really want to make amends, you should let us out," Xellen said sharply. "Otherwise all this talk is useless."

"I don't have a key. But I promise I will try to find a way to get you out. This… This isn't right." He bent down, fumbling with something before he pushed a bundle of cloth through the bars. "Food," he said, gesturing to the bundle as he stood again. "Proper food, anyway."

"Thank you," Orelia said with a measure more gratitude than Xellen felt at the moment. She'd like to have torn the knight's eyes out. He knew that man meant Orelia harm, and yet he'd done nothing to protect her. "But what about Remo?" Orelia asked.

"What about him? He's a madman."

"Granted, but he must be following orders or concocted some kind of plan for the younger Lord Boni to go along with his uncle being murdered in cold blood at his doorstep."

Cirino threw up his hands. "Wouldn't that be deposition? Boni would hardly be the first noble killed for their title."

"Why involve Remo, a complete stranger and a knight sworn to serve His Majesty, in a family affair like this?"

"Is he a complete stranger, though?"

Orelia opened her mouth, then paused. "I suppose he might not be, but why involve our entire conroi, then, and risk exposure of his plot?"

"We offer military strength if we join ranks," Cirino suggested, brows knitting as he puzzled it over. "Maybe he is planning to annex some of the surrounding lands?"

"Or another estate." Orelia chewed her lip, but there was little she could do from inside a cage. "See what you can find out."

"I'll do what I can," the knight sighed, scrubbing at his face. "I have to go. I'll be patrolling until nightfall. I'll try to come back as soon as I can."

"Wait—" Xellen called out when Cirino started to turn on his heel. "Can you bring us anything else?"

The knight's frown deepened. "Like what?"

"Tools? Weapons? We can hide them under the nesting box." When the knight didn't respond, the harpy tried again. "At least some cloth or blankets. It's cold, and a little bit of straw on the floor isn't going to keep us warm while winter settles in."

"Blankets," Cirino repeated. "Sure. I'm sure no one could protest that."

"Thank you," Xellen said, inclining her head as politely as she could manage.

He returned the gesture, glancing around a last time before starting down the path again. It wasn't until the knight was nearly out of sight that Xellen dared turn to Orelia again. "I don't know if I trust him."

"No," Orelia agreed. "But I don't think we have

another choice."

"If you think it's a good idea, I trust you." Bending, Xellen picked up the bundle the knight had left them. Picking the wrapping open, she was pleasantly surprised to find two small pies snugged within. She took a cautious sniff, mouth turning wryly. "Chicken."

"It smells amazing," Orelia sighed.

"I can't remember the last time I had pastry," Xellen admitted, carefully guiding Orelia back up into the nest box.

"Me either. Remo kept us on strict rations while we traveled."

Xellen's feathers stood on end at the mention of that man, the stink of rotten offal still clung faintly in her nose, furious that the man had done much the same to Orelia. Uaris be blessed, but they had to get out of this cage. She didn't know how yet, but she had to get out and take Orelia away from this place—from these men—and show her there were better people out there, people who would understand her and love her the way Xellen had loved her every day since that morning all those years ago. The way she had even after she broke Orelia's heart making the biggest mistake she'd ever come to regret.

Chapter Nine

Orelia's eyes snapped open, the last part of her dream lingering on like an afterimage from staring at the sun—Remo's face, snarling at her as he plunged his sword into her. Gods, how many times did she have to see his face?

She lifted a hand, resisting the impulse to press it to her tender new scar, and pushed the hair from her eyes. Her skin was damp, her clothes sticking to her as if she'd just climbed from a lake. She wrinkled her nose. She must have sweated out the fever, but at least her head was no longer pounding.

"Oh, you're awake." Xellen ducked in the entrance of the nesting box and pressed the back of her hand to Orelia's forehead. "How are you feeling?"

"Better," Orelia answered, her voice a parched croak. Whatever fever had gripped her seemed to be gone, but without its ache, she was all the more aware of how her skin chafed and itched.

"Good. I'm glad." The harpy retracted her hand and

offered a cool, wet rag. "Here. I wish there was more I could do, but I thought you might want to get cleaned up. It will help you feel better."

Sitting up, Orelia took the rag, grimacing as she caught sight of her feet. Gods, they were ugly—twisted and cracked and bloody with half-formed nails.

She started with her face, wiping the sweat and dirt from her forehead. It felt incredible—until the fibers of the cloth snagged on the stubble growing in on her chin, and she felt her stomach lurch.

"Are you all right?" Xellen asked, and Orelia pointedly moved on gingerly wiping her neck.

"You wouldn't happen to have a razor, would you?"

The harpy wilted. "No. I'm sorry. Should I…" Her eyes darted nervously towards Orelia's legs then at the roof before she turned her back to her. "I'll just step outside and keep watch while you clean up," she said quickly, moving into the doorway for the box and spreading her wings, closing Orelia in.

Orelia considered herself, the dried, cracked skin below her knees and the jutting black quills showing beneath her clothes, pinching and itching with every slight movement. The thought of undressing sent a violent jolt of anxiety through her that nearly brought her to tears, but every little twitch and breath made her want to claw her skin open.

Taking a long, slow breath, she set her rag aside, closed her eyes, and began to unfasten the laces of her gambeson, only to falter when she reached the bloody hole torn through her middle by Remo's sword. She had sworn the last time was the final time he would ever lay hands on her, and the bastard went and...

The room swayed, and Orelia caught herself against the wall, forcing herself to take another deep breath and set her hands back to the last few laces. Remo wouldn't get away with this. He would get what he deserved. She would make certain of it.

She let the gambeson drop to the floor and peeled her tunic up over her head, gasping as the coarse fabric scratched across her unexpectedly tender chest.

"Orelia?" Xellen called, but the knight didn't answer, running her hand over her chest.

Ignoring the strange texture of the angry bumps along her skin and minding more the shape and give of her chest, it almost felt...

Orelia looked down, gently cupping her chest, hissing again at the tender ache. It would have hardly been noticeable to anyone other than her, but no. She wasn't imagining it. "Gior...Xell?" She looked up at the harpy, hardly able to draw breath as Xellen looked back at her. "What—I have..." She massaged her chest again, feeling the gentle swell beneath her palms. "I..." Her voice caught in her throat. She had breasts. They were small, but they were definitely there.

"That's..." Xellen peered at her shyly, her small hand lifting to her lips in surprise. "Orelia, you..."

Orelia's breath hitched, and she felt her eyes welling. "Is... Will there be more...ch-changes?"

"Maybe." Hesitantly, Xellen crawled towards her, her wings shielding them from sight, and gently cupped

Orelia's face. "I hope so, though."

Orelia leaned into the touch, tears rolling down her cheeks. Who knew the gods had to take such a price to answer a prayer?

It was heartwarming to see Orelia so happy. She deserved some measure of happiness after everything she had been through just since they had reunited.

"You're going to be a beautiful harpy," she murmured, stroking her thumb over the arch of Orelia's cheek along her pin feathers. "If you… If you're comfortable with it, I can help you with your pin feathers when you're finished washing. You'll feel much—"

The rattle of wheels over stone broke through the subtle, constant noise of the menagerie, and Xellen whirled to place herself in the entrance of the box, wings spread to hide Orelia as a wagon drew near.

"Ah, my beautiful harpy." The young Lord Boni dismounted from a handsome horse, tossing his reins to a guard standing nearby to approach the cage. He smiled, his eyes raking over her, and Xellen's feathers bristled. "I have a special treat for you today." He held up a golden collar, wrought in handsome filigree, but there was no disguising its purpose.

Xellen shrank back, the blood draining from her face even as she bared her teeth.

"Now, now. If you behave and look pretty for my guests, I promise to see to it that you and your…mate are made more comfortable. I can have my handlers bring you proper beds, blankets, cushions. Even hot food. What do you think of that?"

Xellen's nose wrinkled in disgust, but beyond the lord, she could see men with ropes and spears. "What is it you want me to do?"

His smile brightened, like a snake trying to charm a sparrow. "Nothing at all. You merely have to attend the hall. You will be brought right back here when it is through."

As if she had a choice. She knew too well the sound of an empty promise. "What about Orelia?"

"The…other harpy?"

"Yes."

He shrugged. "He isn't needed. Only you, my dear."

Xellen's skin crawled at the pet name. It made her feel naked and filthy, and she wished for the first time in years that she had clothes to cover herself with.

"What do you say?"

Xellen twisted to look back at Orelia, now dressed in her tunic again. "Stay here."

"Gior—Xellen, don't go." Orelia dragged herself forward, her feet still curled in useless contractions. "You don't know—"

"I do know," Xellen said, voice heavy with old pain she hoped Orelia never knew. "I'll be fine. I have talons now." She tapped one of her long, curved nails against the boards, gouging a runnel into the wood. "They won't try it more than once." She turned away from Orelia's stricken face, screwing up her courage even as her heart thudded in her chest, and walked down the ramp to face the lord. "All right. I'll come with you."

"Excellent." The man clapped his hands, turning to his handlers. "Please escort her to the hall, and be gentle. I don't want to see a feather harmed."

The men said nothing, moving mechanically towards the cage door, and for a brief, fluttering moment, Xellen saw a chance to escape. She could rush past them and take wing, fly back to her roost with her flock. But Orelia would still be here, trapped and alone. She'd have to find another way. Xellen wasn't leaving Orelia behind. Not again. Not ever again.

She stood perfectly still as the men set their spear points to her throat and belly as a third man slipped a rope around her neck, jerking it taut. Only then did the door slide open, and one young, nervous-looking guard approached her with manacles. Her feathers bristled, but she held still, even as the guard timidly knelt in front of her and clasped the heavy iron around each of her ankles.

With a tug, she was led by the rope around her neck into the wagon, where she was tied off to a bolt at the center, forcing her to squat low as her head was held down. She twitched away as one of the guards climbed in next to her, a low hiss scraping over her teeth. She wasn't some defenseless country girl anymore, she reminded herself, locking eyes with the man. She was a harpy.

The wagon lurched into motion, and she dug her talons into the wood to steady herself as it rocked and bounced. She heard the creak of a gate, and found herself suddenly breathing cool night air beneath the stars. She gulped it down, gazing up at the gods' menagerie where she would be free to fly one day, a glittering light amongst her sisters that had come before her and would come after.

All too soon, the wagon rolled under another archway, and the night sky was replaced by the vaulted ceilings of one of Great Houses. They came to a stop, and there was a flurry of motion as the guards dismounted and consulted with servants that seemed to appear from nowhere. One of the men untied her rope from the center of the wagon, and she was led from what appeared to be a well-hidden alcove into the strangest dining hall she had ever laid eyes upon.

At the very center of the room was what appeared to be a glittering tree wrought of brightly polished brass, its twisting limbs carefully crafted to give the illusion of natural chaos while forming a sturdy place for someone—or something—to sit quite comfortably. Around it were tables lavishly arrayed with trays of steaming food—meats in rich sauces, pastries, bread, fruits, even tureens of vegetables loaded with spices. Xellen's stomach let out a plaintive growl.

The guard holding her rope walked her over to the tree, watching her warily as he looped her rope through another tie point. "Up you go, bird."

Biting her tongue, Xellen climbed up the tree, using the discrete handholds to reach the perch. She had no more settled into the cup of the branches than a pair of doors at the far end of the hall swung open to admit the Lord Boni, flanked by the knight Remo and another man dressed in bright finery she didn't recognize, trailed by the rest of the knights that had betrayed Orelia. Her feathers stood on end, a low, feline growl rumbling in her chest.

The three men stopped in front of her, peering up curiously, before the man she didn't recognize let out a rumble of laughter. "You brought a harpy into your home?"

"Yes," the lordling said proudly. "The knight commander and his conroi captured it."

The man cocked his head, stepping towards her. He was smaller than the other two men, his blond hair and fair skin quite the contrast to Remo's black and silver he kept clubbed at his neck or the Lord Boni's rich, golden brown coif. "You are either foolish or fearless," he remarked, his eyes flicking up to catch Xellen's with a scouring intensity that made her cover herself.

"And why is that?" the lordling demanded, a note of petulance in his voice.

"You have invited a servant of death into your noble house and feign to bind it."

"Feign?" Lord Boni scoffed. "I assure you she is quite contained."

The man grinned, showing the glint of metal amongst his teeth. "We shall see."

"So we shall," the lordling sniffed. "Let us dine now before supper grows cold with waiting."

The man's shoulders moved in a silent laugh and he

finally turned away. "Very well."

Xellen didn't miss the way Remo watched the man, a look of distaste writ into his features. They settled at the table directly before her, and the rest of the knights spread out amongst the other tables. Xellen could feel their eyes on her from every direction, and she crouched on her perch, wrapping her wings as tightly around herself as she could, but it didn't seem to matter. All around her, she could hear their lewd remarks and vile imaginations of things they would like to do to her. Worst of all was when they started imagining it of Orelia too.

"Blessed Uaris, protect us," she whispered, covering her ears and closing her eyes to all of it.

Chapter Ten

Orelia lay in the nest box for as long as she could suffer until the idleness threatened to drive her mad. There was nothing to distract her from the heady tangle of her heart and mind. Despite her circumstances, she couldn't help running her hands softly over her chest, feeling the gentle, but definite swell of her breasts. She almost wished she had a mirror, but couldn't bring herself to look at the rest of her new body yet, too frightened by what she might find—or might not find.

Would she look like Xellen once the change was over? All soft curves covered in golden brown down and feathers? She doubted it. Orelia was all gangling limbs and towering angles where Xellen had always been soft and sweet, especially her lips when they…

Orelia shook her head. Those days had passed. Xellen had given her a clear answer that day. There was no point yearning for things to be different. She knew better than most that feelings never did amount to change.

Chewing her lip, Orelia cautiously got to her feet. Hand at the wall, she took a wobbling step, knees bent, her balance tottering. She felt like she was going to pitch over backwards balancing on toes that wouldn't set flat, but she was determined not to simply lay about and wait any longer.

She took a cautious step away from the support of the wall, high stepping down the ramp around the awkward shape of her changing feet. By some miracle she reached the bottom, grimacing at the rough stone floor against her cracked and bleeding skin. What she wouldn't give for a bit of grass, of all things.

When she reached the bars, she leaned heavily against them, peering out and taking in the fine mosaic composed of animals of every kind. She couldn't see any of the other cages, blocked by the archway her prison was set in behind, but she could hear them— strange cries, calls, and bellows. No rattle of a wagon, though.

Reluctantly, she turned her attention inward, to the bars themselves as she began to pace along them. She hoped to find a weakness. Some poor craftsmanship, or place where a previous occupant had damaged them. Anything. Anywhere she might be able to make an opening. There was no telling how or when Cirino might decide to help them, and that could be too late for whatever Remo was up to. She would have to find her own way out. She had fought hard for her knighthood, and she would not break those sacred vows now. Even in death.

Their cage was well made, though. Flecks of rust spotted the metal where the bars met the ground, but the bars themselves were strong and unbending everywhere she tried pulling at them. Until…

Clink.

Orelia gave the bar in her hand another firm yank. It wiggled and shifted, hardly more than a hair's breadth, but it was a start. She tried the others around it, but they didn't budge. She tried the first again, bracing and yanking as hard as she could, but it didn't shift any further. She needed leverage. Maybe one of the boards from the ramp or nest?

Another sound caught her attention and she looked down the walking path again, spotting the approaching guard in the distance, his head turning to look towards their cage. Spitting a sharp curse, Orelia let go of the bar, pacing forwards along the outside of their cage until she was mostly hidden behind the nest box, waiting until the clink of the guard's buckles faded from hearing again.

She eased into motion, circling and searching relentlessly as the evening crawled by. She kept hoping to find more. A place where the iron had been set badly. A faulty lock. A tool left forgotten and unattended. As it was, she had one loose bar, a few small rocks, and an irritatingly unpredictable guard route.

There was a different sort of noise from the path, and Orelia caught a glimpse of guards and a wagon, and withdrew into the nest box. She watched as they untied

Xellen from the back of the wagon and towed her into the entrance of the cage. She considered rushing out when they opened the gate, but with no weapons and her body caught in the middle of its change, not to mention the irons on Xellen's legs, she wasn't confident they could make a clean escape. And she doubted she'd come back from another sword through her belly.

Shrinking into the dark, she ran her fingers over her middle, tracing the angry, barbed bumps that had welted along her entire body. But she felt no hole, only an uneven puckering, like a bad scar.

"Orelia?"

Orelia sighed at the familiar voice, at the things it still did to her all these years later. "In here," she said, peering out of the box, the wagon rattling away. Xellen looked much as she had before they had led her away, minus some rumbled feathers at her throat and ankles from her bonds. But something was clearly wrong. "What happened?"

Xellen shook her head, seeming to shrink in on herself. "Nothing. He had me sit at their supper in a tree…" Her voice cracked, breath hitching, and she hid her face behind her wings. "Remo was there with him, and another man."

"One of the knights?" Orelia asked, carefully making her way down the ramp to Xellen's side.

The harpy shook her head, raising her head just far enough to show the tears rolling down her cheeks. "No. He was dressed like another noble." She described the man, but he didn't sound like any of the nobles Orelia had ever studied in her schooling. Which left an unnerving alternative—someone from beyond the borders.

"Was he…?" Orelia's question trailed off as she looked at Xellen's teary face. She reached to cup her cheek, brushing the curly strands of Xellen's hair from her eyes. "Are you sure you're all right?"

"Mhmm," Xellen mumbled, managing a nod before she crumpled into a sob.

"Come here." Orelia pulled her into her arms, squeezing her as tightly as she dared.

"I'm fine," Xellen whimpered, burying her face in the crook of Orelia's neck. "I'm all right. They didn't— They didn't touch me."

"That doesn't—Look at you," she reasoned, slowly sinking to the ground, pulling Xellen with her until the harpy was curled in her lap. "What did they do to you?"

The harpy shuddered, her fingers balling in Orelia's tunic. "They…made me sit in a tree while they ate…so they could—could *look* at me."

Orelia's belly dropped between her knees. "Gods, those sick—I'm sorry. I'm so sorry." She clenched and unclenched her fists, fighting the urge to grab the bars of their cage and scream until one of those guards got close enough she could grab him by the throat and squeeze.

"I'll get you out of here," Orelia said, gently rocking Xellen in her arms. "I'll find a way soon. I promise." Even if it meant only getting *her* out.

Chapter Eleven

It was sometime later that Xellen lay curled with Orelia in the nesting box. She'd been fighting to keep her eyes open, but sleep must have won. "Hello," she mumbled, trying to curl closer, but she was all but wrapped around the knight.

Orelia's face crinkled sweetly. "Hello." Xellen blinked heavily, soaking in the strength of the arms around her, and the soft tickle of Orelia's breath on her cheek, their legs tangled. She didn't remember climbing the ramp, but here she was, staring sleepily into Orelia's gentle smile. "How long…?" She stifled a yawn.

"Just a few hours," Orelia assured her, her fingers petting one of Xellen's long flight feathers.

"Oh." She worried at a thick shafted pin with her thumb and forefinger, her teeth finding her lip. "I'm supposed to be the one comforting and protecting you now."

Orelia twitched and caught her hand, cupping Xellen's fingers. "Tickles."

Xellen's heart tried to jump into her throat, and she giggled girlishly. "Let me help then. You'll feel better once we preen them all." She wiggled her fingers in Orelia's grasp until, with a gentle squeeze, the knight let her hand go.

"I don't suppose they'll open on their own?" Orelia sighed, her eyes slipping closed as Xellen pinched a tiny pin at her hairline, releasing a tiny, pale down feather.

"No. If we were at the roost, the flock would help you with this all together. There'd be food of every kind. Cream for your skin to ease the itching. Drink for your nerves. Gifts to adorn your nest. It's always a special event to mark the birth of a newcomer."

She let herself brush her knuckles across Orelia's cheek, taking in the face she remembered so well and the changes that had come in the years since they'd parted. There were lines that hadn't been there before, little scars of time worn in around her eyes and across her forehead, and she was so much more serious and quiet than the girl she'd first met chasing her puppy.

"What's it like to live there?"

Xellen pulled herself from her memories, smiling. "It's wonderful. Like a big family. We share duties for chores like hunting, weaving, and brewing, and we take our meals together."

Orelia pursed her lips. "Sounds a lot like my conroi."

Xellen's feathers bristled. "The flock would never turn on one of its own."

"I didn't mean that. I only meant that it sounded similar to what life as a knight was supposed to be. We were supposed to be brothers at arms." Her mouth twisted into a grimace, her eyes going flat and hard. "I should have expected as much after my own family turned me out."

The harpy's fingers stilled around a pin feather she had been worrying. "What do you mean?"

"Precisely what I said. After you were married off, my father gave me an ultimatum. Marry someone respectable to produce an heir for the family and cease my scandalous, *unnatural* behavior, or I would no longer be a Sanctis."

Xellen's eyes went perfectly round. "He what?"

"I didn't want either, so I asked about until I found someone I could beg for a commendation and left for the capital to become a knight. My father wasn't happy, but since it was considered *noble* to serve your king and country, he didn't openly object. Not until the rumors of the Lady Knight of Vizeras reached him." She smiled bitterly. "I received his letter telling me not to come home about the same time I got the one from your mother explaining you had passed in an accident."

An *accident*. Xellen tried not to feel a surge of resentment. After the threats, the guilt, all of the misery, to call it just an accident felt so…

Perhaps she shouldn't be surprised. Not after her family had been willing to sell her to repair their reputation. But for Orelia's family to cast her out like that. "That's monstrous."

"It's what happens to people like me in this life." She rested her forehead against Xellen's. "Like us. You would have been cast out with me if you hadn't set me straight that day, I know that now, and I'm sorry I said those things back then."

Xellen's throat closed up as she thought of that final day. "I wish I'd known what would come," she whispered.

Slowly, Orelia shook her head. "Don't we all?"

"Yes, but—"

There was a clack against the bars outside. Orelia shot up, moving between Xellen and the opening of the box.

The harpy crawled behind her, peeking warily around Orelia until she caught sight of tightly coiled locks. "Cirino?"

The knight held up a pair of rough spun blankets that looked to have never seen a wash basin in the last decade. "I pinched these from the stables. It's the best I could do."

"A pair of horse blankets?" Orelia snorted drily.

"They'll keep you warm." He seemed to waver, waiting for Orelia to say something, but she was stonily silent. Hesitantly, he sank to his knee and passed the blankets through the bars, nestling something amidst the folds. "I was told to bring the harpy for the next meal."

The air vanished from Xellen's lungs. "No," she wheezed, her chest heaving, but she just couldn't pull down enough air. "No, I can't—"

"She's not an ornament," she heard Orelia snap.

"That's not…she…"

Cirino's answer faded in and out, drowned beneath a rushing, ringing that seemed to fill Xellen's ears.

"Xellen?"

Her knees wobbled and she clutched Orelia's tunic. "I…"

"I've got you," came Orelia's warm, comforting voice, cutting through the storm rushing in Xellen's head. "I've got you."

"He's going to… I don't… I can't…"

"Just breathe." A weight settled over Xellen's chest, moving with her breaths. "Breathe with me."

Xellen heard the knight draw a deep breath, and tried to take one too, but it still felt so inadequate, like she was drowning on land. "I…" There was another breath, and she tried to match it again. Slowly, steadily, eyes shut to everything but the sound of Orelia's breath and the soothing murmur of her voice, Xellen's heart finally began to slow.

"There's my girl." There was a ghost of a kiss against the top of her head, and she felt a squeeze at her hand. "Will you be all right to stay right here?"

"Wha—?"

"I'll be right back. I'm just going to go ask Cirino a *question.*"

The threat in her voice almost pulled a chuckle from Xellen. "I… Yes. I'm all right now. Thank you." Even so, it felt like she was losing part of herself as Orelia's arms slipped from around her, and the knight stalked down the ramp.

"You can tell the new Lord Boni that Xellen is ill

and won't be in attendance," Orelia sneered.

"It—" Cirino glanced around, wetting his lips before he leaned towards the bars. "It was not the lord that requested her presence, but the other man, Léonce Daviau."

Orelia stiffened. "Why do I know that name?"

"He is a *Seduí* mercenary. He has offered his and his army's support to anyone able to pay his fee. Boni and Remo want to use his men to bolster their numbers and take down the other noble houses and the Crown."

Orelia sucked down a breath. "They've both gone mad. We have to stop them."

"I can get you out tonight, but all I can do is open the cage. You'll have to get yourselves out of here."

Orelia looked back at Xellen, her face set in a grim determination. "I can do that."

"Until then, it's best if you both cooperate—"

"No," Orelia cut him off, and Xellen wet her lips. She didn't want to go, but if this was their best chance…

"I'll go," she said weakly, clenching her fists until they shook.

Orelia's anger softened with concern as she looked up at Xellen, lurching into motion as if to go to her. "Are you sure?"

Xellen raised her chin, trying to be braver than she felt. "I'll go and sit in his tree and I'll rob the coins from his eyes one day before he can cross the sea."

Orelia bared her teeth in a grin. "I'll be sure to send him soon."

Chapter Twelve

Orelia crouched, pensive and impatient, in the opening of the nesting box, watching as the shadows grew longer and deeper in the menagerie. Xellen lay asleep behind her, making so little noise, Orelia had to glance back to be certain she was breathing. The harpy had been quiet after her return from attending the lord's second supper, though she assured Orelia that none of them had laid a hand on her, nor said anything useful in front of her. She wouldn't elaborate more than that, and Orelia's thoughts darkened as she imagined what they likely conversed about. Bastards, one and all.

She scratched at the floorboard with one clawed toe, hoping to splinter off a piece she might use as a weapon. It was difficult and strange to manage, the very sight of the long, arching talons causing her stomach to turn somersaults, but she had no better ideas to arm herself, and her fingers were useless. She held out her hand, examining the bruised, bloody nail beds where the barest tips of new nails were growing in. They ached almost as badly as her chest and belly. A dull cramping pain had started in her midsection earlier. She put it down as hunger, given how little they had been fed, but it did nothing to lessen the gnawing discomfort.

The shadows had stretched and melted into dark pools before she heard a patrol that didn't sound like one of the guards. She eased forward, staring at the wisp of torchlight as it grew brighter and closer, and Cirino rounded the corner of the archway. But as Orelia moved to meet him at the front of the cage, he turned away and kept walking, disappearing from view again.

"Hey!" she hissed, rattling the bars. "Get back here!"

But the warm light of his torch faded from view, leaving Orelia and Xellen still trapped inside their cage.

"Bastard," Orelia sneered, stalking back up to the nest box. If he had gotten cold feet and intended to abandon their plan, she would make sure he didn't walk away the next time he came within reach.

But as she kept vigilance, she saw Cirino pass several more times along with other guards, and she finally put together that he was making rounds and waiting for an opportunity to approach without being seen. With a grumble, she settled in to wait, pinching at her pin feathers to pass the time.

It wasn't until the early hours of the morning that she saw him creep into the archway, no torch in hand, feeling along the wall until his hand landed on the mechanism for the door. Orelia leaned forward, hardly daring to breathe as he looked up at her and with a nod, pulled the mechanism.

"Thank the gods," Orelia whispered, reaching for the harpy. "Xellen—"

"I'm awake," she said, crawling to Orelia's side. "He did it."

"He did," Orelia echoed, glancing back into the archway, but the knight was already gone. "Let's go. Stay close and quiet. Stick to the shadows."

They hurried through the open pair of doors, following the wall to the archway. Orelia cringed at the clicking of their nails against the mosaic stone, but there was nothing for it. Gesturing for Xellen to stay behind her, she leaned out of the archway, peering left and right at the distant light of torches moving through the menagerie, reflecting off the many, many eyes of the other restless creatures.

"Ready?" she whispered to Xellen.

Slipping her hand into Orelia's and squeezing gently, the harpy nodded.

With a deep breath to settle her nerves, Orelia slipped out of the protective cover of their archway. She kept them to the shadows, never getting too close or too far from the torchlight ahead of them. Creatures stirred as they passed, hissing and lowing as they paced within their bars.

She grit her teeth and crouched in the shadow of one archway that led to a cage housing what she could only guess was a manticore from the illustrations she had seen at the Crown's library during her training. The low rumble of its growl sent chills down her spine, its scorpion tail striking the bars with a hard crash of rock against iron, venom frothing from the tip. But as terrifying as it was, she couldn't help but pity the creature, trapped in such a small cage for however long it might live for the amusement of a few nobles that wished to gaze upon it.

"Oye, you! Shut it!"

Orelia flinched at the sudden slurring voice from close by, pressing against the wall as tightly as she could with Xellen. The harpy's grip tightened around her fingers as a guard staggered upright from the other side of the archway. Orelia cursed silently. The idiot had been sleeping off his drink instead of making his rounds, and she hadn't even noticed him.

The manticore let out a deafening roar, its human-like eyes locking on the guard as its fur bristled.

The guard didn't even flinch. "Stupid beast," he mumbled, fumbling with his belt. "Was just tryin' to—" He drifted forwards, unfastening to ties of his breeches, then came to a dead stop. He stiffened then, slowly, raised his head to look right at Orelia. They stared at one another, both frozen in place until the guard's mouth opened.

Orelia lunged for him, only to be brought up short by Xellen. "Wait!"

"Escape!" the guard bellowed, tripping over his boots as he tried to get away. "There's been a—"

"Xellen, he's—"

There was a clack and rattle of a mechanism being

activated, and Orelia could only watch in horror as the cage doors swung open. With a deep, primal bellow, the manticore sprang from its cage, claws and teeth bared, and threw the guard screaming to the ground.

"Go," Xellen whispered just loud enough to be heard over the man's awful screams as the manticore savaged him. "The others will be coming."

Orelia tore her eyes from the sight, but she couldn't shut out the sounds as she fled the scene, her stomach lurching up into her throat. Xellen pulled her into another alcove as a pair of guards went racing by to help their fallen comrade. "You… It—"

"He would have taken us back," Xellen said firmly, brushing a strand of hair from Orelia's sweat-sheened face. "We have to keep going while they're distracted."

Orelia nodded, swallowing her bile. This was no time to be squeamish. These men conspired to kill the Lord Boni and allied themselves with Remo. They were traitors.

Taking Xellen's hand again, Orelia pulled them from the alcove. She could see the exit now, the doors thrown wide to let in the night air. Moonlight spilled across the mosaic tiles, brilliant and white, and she could almost taste the night breeze. Then one of the doors slammed shut, a shadow occluding the entrance as another guard crossed to swing the other shut. If they closed those, there would be no escape. They would be trapped in the menagerie and forced back into their cage. There wouldn't be another chance to escape.

Pumping her arms, Orelia broke into a sprint, racing

for the doors, when her middle seized with a cramp that stole her breath away. She staggered, fighting to keep moving forward as her vision narrowed to a black tunnel and she retched on the tiles.

A flash of golden brown went streaking by her, and she managed to raise her head just enough to see Xellen, wings tucked tight and hair streaming black and silver in the moonlight as she flew through the shrinking gap between the doors. The thud of an impact and a wet scream pealed through the night before it cut off abruptly.

Cursing her body, Orelia dragged herself forward, terrified of what she might find just outside when she had to catch herself against the solid wood as her insides tried to turn themselves inside out. "Gods, why now?" she pleaded silently, spitting onto the cobbles as she retched again. "Xell—?"

"I'm here." The harpy's arms slid around her, pulling her away from the door. "What's happening? Are you all right?"

A sharp, lightning bolt of pain shot down between Orelia's thighs from her aching middle, and only Xellen's grip on her kept her upright. It felt like she was dying. Something was wrong. "I'll be fine," she gritted through her teeth. "We've got to get out of here before—"

"Sound the alarm!"

Orelia lifted her head to see a guard pelting across the grounds towards the estate.

"There's been an escape!"

Gathering herself, Orelia forced her legs to carry her forward. If she was going to die again, it wasn't going to be because she laid down and let them take her. She would fight before she let them have her again. "The forest. If we can make the trees…" Then, Xellen might be able to get away while she made a stand. Then, at least, it all wouldn't be for nothing.

Chapter Thirteen

The trees seemed miles away as Xellen half-supported, half-dragged Orelia out of the garden and across the open lawn. The knight shuddered against her, sweat pouring down her pale face as she dry-heaved every few steps. This wasn't part of the change, at least as far as Xellen remembered. It must be something else, some illness, or…

Xellen's blood chilled. A poison could do this. Someone could have given Orelia something when Xellen wasn't there. And if—

The sound of shouts growing louder interrupted the panicked swirl of her thoughts. She glanced over her shoulder to see a group of men with torches pointing their direction as a rider galloped past them, thundering towards the harpy and the knight.

She sucked in a breath. "Oh, Uaris."

Orelia looked back, her expression grim. "Can you fly?"

"Yes, but—"

"Good." The knight pulled out of her arms, turning to face the rider. She stood hunched, one arm around her middle, her hair and clothes plastered to her skin, and face set in grim determination. "I'll distract him. See if you can knock him out of his seat."

Xellen's protest that she wouldn't leave Orelia behind fizzled on her tongue. She looked between rider and knight, frightened for what Orelia might be about to do, but she had no better plan. Crouching low, she spread her wings and sprang into the air, veering to one side as she struggled to gain height.

"Damn birds!" the rider bellowed as he bore down on them, a bola whistling in his hand.

A shock of fear lanced through Xellen's belly, recalling all too keenly the cutting grip of the bola's ropes around her wings, when Orelia let out a deafening shriek. Arms waving, eyes wide, and teeth bared, Orelia ran screaming straight at the rider.

Xellen banked, tucking her wings close, in time to see the rider's steed throw its head up, eyes round and white, and veer away from Orelia. Cursing, the rider yanked on the reins, trying to take back control, and so didn't see Xellen as she stretched out her talons and collided with him.

He tumbled from his seat, hitting the ground with a loud snap of breaking bone as he rolled across the lawn, his mount thundering on. Xellen alighted just as Orelia shouldered by, planting her heel across the man's temple. His head snapped back, blood streaming down his face. Orelia bent over him, drawing his sword and tearing the bola from his hand.

"Stay back," she said brusquely, starting after the steed.

The horse slowed to a stop, tail twitching, and hooves stamping nervously. Orelia approached it at a steady pace and caught its reins before the horse could back away, swinging up into the saddle with surprisingly easy grace. Guiding it back around, she halted it next to Xellen and held out a hand.

The horse seemed so much bigger from the ground than it had from the air, and Xellen eyed it nervously as it shifted and stomped. "I don't know how to ride."

"That's all right. I won't let you fall."

Xellen smiled faintly and, setting her hand in Orelia's, leapt as the knight pulled, settling in the saddle in front of Orelia. One of Orelia's arms wrapped firmly around Xellen's waist, pulling her tightly against the knight's chest, warm, and firm, and unmistakably feminine, and despite everything, a blush kindled across Xellen's cheeks.

Orelia guided their horse towards the road leading into the woods, urging it faster until they were galloping over the ground and into the dark of the woods. Xellen clung to the horse's mane, terrified and thrilled as trees flashed by on either side. She'd only ever gone this fast when diving off the flock's roost, waiting until the last minute to spread her wings and catch the updraft to carry her into the sky.

They kept going, on and on, twisting through the woods until they came to a fork in the path. Orelia pulled hard on the reins, her arm around Xellen's middle holding firm as the horse skidded to a sudden stop. "Down. Quickly," the knight ordered, changing her grip to Xellen's arm. The harpy swung her leg over and dropped to the ground, staggering away on shaky knees. "Fly up into one of the trees and hide there until they pass."

Xellen leaned against a craggy rock, a new thrill of fear lighting through her. "What about you?"

"I'll lead them away. It will buy you time to get away."

"No," Xellen said firmly. "I won't leave you to those monsters."

Orelia glanced down the road behind them. "It might be the only way—"

"Well, find another way. I'm *not* abandoning you."

The knight's lips parted in a little 'oh' of surprise, and she flicked another glance back down the road. "Fine. Find a place to hide. I'll lead them down this path then regroup with you."

Xellen bit her lip. That sounded an awful lot like the same plan, but she didn't have any ideas herself. She'd just have to trust the knight. "All right. But you better come back to me."

Orelia smiled, her eyes crinkling warmly. "Every time." Kicking her horse, she took off down the road, leaving Xellen standing at the fork, and for not the first time, Xellen wondered if this was how Orelia felt that day at the lake.

Orelia spurred her horse on, fleeing as fast and far down the road as she could without losing her seat. She hunched over her mount's neck, giving the steed its head and trying not to vomit at the pain wracking her. It felt like someone had shoved a hot metal rod through her middle and twisted it.

She had no idea how she was going to keep her promise to Xellen she had stupidly made. She hadn't meant to make it, but she couldn't think of anything else in the moment to get Xellen to comply

When she gauged she had gone far enough, she reined in her mount and let herself fall out of the saddle to her feet. The ground was hard and dry, and she moved her feet carefully to avoid scratching up the dirt with her clawed toes. With a hard slap, she sent the horse down the road, and clambered up the embankment into the brush. The forest floor was thick with fallen needles and prickly bushes. Dropping to her knees, she crawled under the thickest parts, branches snagging at her face, hair, and clothes. She found a low spot beneath a dense thicket and curled up to wait just as the sound of thundering hooves raced up the road.

She peered past the covering branches, just catching a glimpse of the knights' newly adopted colors flashing by. She turned her face into the soil, holding her breath until they had passed, the sound of their hooves fading into the distance.

With a soft groan, Orelia dragged herself from the brush back to the road and started back the way she had come as quickly as she could manage.

It was an age before she finally found the branch in the path again. She'd hardly set foot on the crux of the path when Xellen dropped down from above.

"They took the bait," Orelia assured her and jerked her chin down the other path. "This way."

Xellen tucked close to her, eyes flitting up and down her, but the harpy didn't say anything of her obvious distress. "Where are we headed?"

"Away," Orelia said simply, because she didn't know. There was nowhere they could go on foot far enough away they wouldn't be caught or turned into the knights. Her only hope was they might go far enough one of Xellen's flock might find her and take her away.

"We should head for the shore. The flock might see us there," Xellen suggested, apparently of the same mind.

"Do you know the way?"

"I know the direction." she pointed confidently at the trees on their left.

Orelia eyed the thick underbrush. "We'll look for a path. Let's go."

They followed the road as quickly as Orelia could manage, the only sound the click of their nails against the hard dirt and rock and Orelia's wheezing breaths. She could feel Xellen watching her as sweat drenched her clothes anew, the fabric sticking to her back, binding around her arms, chest, and thighs. She wanted to claw it all off.

They stopped when they came to a stream, and

drank. The water was cold and clear, but sour from the fallen needles. Orelia couldn't manage more than a few sips before she simply splashed it over her face and neck. She shivered. It felt incredible.

"This way," she said at last, leading them downstream, keeping to the deeper parts where there was more sand and rocks than mud. Hopefully it would hide their tracks well enough.

She took the first deer path they found, winding through the trees. It was difficult to navigate in the dark, and she had to keep stopping to pluck spider webs from her face and catch her breath.

"We could stop," Xellen suggested at one point, watching as Orelia propped herself against a tree to clutch her middle. "Just for a little while."

Orelia shook her head. "No, I—"

The sound of hounds baying in the distance sent her pulse leaping, and Orelia shot upright. "We have to go. Now!"

They raced along the trail, swiping aside webs and snagging thorns that opened fiery lines of red across their cheeks and arms. Then, at last, the brush parted and before them was a barren rocky expanse and the silvery expanse of the sea.

"We made it," Xellen whispered breathlessly.

But the sound of the hounds only grew louder behind them.

"Come on." Orelia took Xellen by the hand and picked her way out amongst the rocks. The path was treacherous with only moonlight to guide them, the craggy cliffs deeply shadowed in every crevice and low point. Her eyes raked over the edge, searching for a path downwards, someplace out of sight and hard to follow where she could make some kind of stand when a pack of hounds burst from the brush behind them.

Orelia cursed, brandishing her stolen sword as two knights appeared behind the pack. Her lip curled in a sneer as she met Remo's eyes. This was it. She was going to put this sword through his shriveled heart or she would die trying before she let them take her back to that cage.

"Orelia! Come with me!" Xellen shouted from behind her, but Orelia shook her off. The harpy could fly. Orelia couldn't.

She tightened her grip on her sword, ready to swing as the first of the hounds drew near when she saw a flicker of movement through the moonlight where the knights had drawn up at the treeline. As she watched, she could just barely make out Remo as he drew his arm back, as if drawing…

A bow.

"No!" She whirled. Xellen was hovering just above her over the lip of the cliff, hand outstretched, completely oblivious to the barbed point aimed at them both. Without thinking, without hesitation, she leapt, wrapping her arms around the harpy, dragging her out of the air as something whistled just past their heads.

And then the horrible rush of the fall caught her, the cliff edge shrinking as the ocean spread out beneath them. She looked into Xellen's terrified, beautiful face and knew.

This was it.

Grabbing the harpy, she kissed her the way she had always dreamed of kissing her, the way she had hoped would change her mind.

And then she let go.

Chapter Fourteen

Xellen's head spun at the press of Orelia's mouth, her thoughts spilling out in a tortured mess. How she had imagined her life when she was young. How she had wished she had been brave enough to steer it. How she still desperately hoped she could change it now.

And then reality came crashing back in as the kiss broke and Orelia disappeared beneath the frothing waves.

"Orelia!" Tucking her arms to her sides, Xellen dove after the knight. The sea was black as ink, the current buffeting and pulling at Xellen as she fought her way down to Orelia. The knight was thrashing against the tide, spun this way and that, dragged across rocks, and smashed into the sea floor. Xellen snatched for something—anything—she could get hold of, and wrapped her fist in Orelia's tunic.

She dragged the knight into her arms, and kicked for the surface only to be caught in the next swirl of the tide and rolled across the bottom. She felt Orelia spasm against her, limbs thrashing, felt bubbles trail from her nose across her face, before something caught them both up and pulled them to the surface.

Xellen gulped the cool night air greedily, clinging to Orelia as the knight coughed and wheezed, and to their savior.

A siren, too dark to make out in the night black water but for a flash of white teeth and a glint of light on flat black eyes, had them in her grasp, her long sinuous form undulating beneath them as she towed them seemingly effortlessly through the rough surf.

"Take a deep breath," the siren said, her voice a low, lilting vibrato.

Xellen sucked down a lungful of air just before the siren dipped beneath the waves, pulling them under. With a powerful surge of her tail, she slipped through a hidden aperture, twisting down a narrow corridor of rock, before surfacing once again within the hidden confines of a sea cave. The tight grip around Xellen's waist loosened and fell away, and the harpy found herself deposited on a beach of rounded pebbles next to Orelia.

"Are we—" Orelia wheezed between hacking coughs, struggling to drag herself up out of the water.

"We're safe," Xellen assured her, pulling her up onto a shelf of stone above the water. The cave was illuminated by a faint blue glow emanating from several pools dug into the pebbles where small schools of brilliantly luminous fish darted to and fro. Squinting, Xellen could just make out the shape of the siren watching them, only her eyes and the very top of her head above the water.

Cupping Orelia's face in her hands, Xellen looked the knight over, but other than a few obvious scrapes, she looked well enough after what they'd been through, if very pale.

"You escaped." The siren's strange voice echoed around the cave, low and sonorous, making Xellen's ears ache.

Orelia's hands curled into fists in the stones. "What—Who is that?"

"Nerinea," the siren answered, rolling forward until she was perched at the bottom of the pebbly shore. Xellen could make out more of her now—the sweet, round face nearly as large as Xellen's chest and belly, the thick, black claws tipping hand-like fins, and hair like a mat of seaweed spread out behind her.

Something tickled at Xellen's memory. "You… You're the siren who keeps stealing our fish."

Nerinea grinned, flashing sharp, conical teeth. "They're the sea's, not yours."

Xellen snorted. "I'm Xellen. This is Orelia."

"A new pretty bird for the flock," the siren murmured, the water stirring behind her. "They've been furious. Stirred up like sand in a storm."

Xellen straightened. "The flock?"

"Flying up and down the coast." There was a splash behind the siren, her head swaying. "Some even braved the forest."

"They're looking for me." The thought gave her a

burst of joy. "Gods, I can't wait to see them again. They'll be so excited to meet you, Orelia."

The knight made a tight smile, folding her arms over her chest with a shiver. "What about Remo?"

"What about him?"

"He'll be looking for us."

"We move by night, then. We'll be hard to see."

"And after that?"

Xellen shifted closer, pressing her shoulder into Orelia's. "The flock is planning to migrate. He won't be able to find us ever again. We'll be safe.

"But what about the people here? Whatever Remo is planning, they won't be safe."

"There are other knights and soldiers. You're not a knight anymore. You don't owe them anything."

Orelia looked at her, brows set in a frown. "They're innocent people."

"Innocent people who didn't protect you. That wouldn't have," Xellen said sharply, the memory of Orelia's face as she died too fresh in her mind. "They would have come to gawk at you and they would kill you if they saw you now." She reached up, touching the knight's cheek to draw her down until their lips nearly brushed. "Please. Please come with me. You can't stop them on your own and I can't bear to watch you die again."

Something wet and warm touched Xellen's cheek, and she opened her eyes to see tears streaking down Orelia's face. She brushed them away with her thumb, pressing a kiss to each of her cheeks. "Please."

"A letter," Orelia finally said. "If I can send a letter to my mentor, he'll believe me."

Xellen's heart quailed. "How are you going to send a letter? If you walk into town…"

"I'll figure it out, if I have to threaten someone to take it."

"I know someone that will help." The siren pulled herself up onto the beach, her shark's eyes glittering from a girl's face. "I'll take you to her."

※

Orelia didn't really want to climb back into the cold, dark water, but there were hardly any other options at this point. She couldn't very well swim the distance herself. Her cramps had subsided to a tolerable level, but had not entirely gone away. She could tell now there were changes happening in her body—more than simply growing feathers—but she couldn't bring herself to look at or feel what they might be, too frightened and self-conscious of what she might find.

So, after a short reprieve on the hidden shore of the sea cave, she and Xellen waded back into the embrace of the massive siren. Nerinea towed them through the chilly water down the coast, keeping close to the shoreline where shadows concealed their passage, until she brought them to a concealed stretch of beach at a place Orelia knew well.

Ahead of them, a familiar old, wiry woman stood on a rotting pier jutting out into the water, loading net into a boat by the light of the distant dawn and stars.

"Stay here," the siren whispered, ushering them beneath a patch of brush overhanging the water, and slipped away.

Orelia knelt shivering in the shallows next to Xellen, keeping her gaze directed on the moving shadow beneath the water so she wouldn't be tempted to think of the kiss she had given the harpy, or Xellen's pleading in the cave that had nearly undone her. Words she had dreamed of hearing the last five years. But why now after all this time, after she was the one that left Orelia?

Nerinea surfaced by the boat, grabbing the edge of the tiny vessel to peer over it at the woman. The old woman dropped the net, clutching her chest before she wagged a finger at the siren, setting her fists to her hips.

"I told you not to do that," she scowled through a dawning smile. "And don't you say you're sorry. I know you meant to scare the last hair off my head."

The siren swayed in the water. "I brought someone to see you, mamma."

"Did you now?" The old woman squinted past Nerinea, scrutinizing the shore and water. "Well, they'd better hurry. It won't be long before someone comes along."

Nerinea turned, beckoning with one clawed fin, and Orelia and Xellen crept from beneath the brush. Orelia saw the woman's expression soften as they grew near, her gaze fixed on Orelia.

"Oh, my poor dear. I'm so sorry."

Xellen glanced at Orelia. "You know each other?"

"I was quartered in her house when my conroi was

113

stationed in this village," Orelia explained quietly. "But I need to ask a favor, Maura."

"What is it, dear?"

"I need to send a letter. It's urgent."

Maura smiled kindly. "Of course. Let me just go and fetch my kit from the house."

They watched as she lifted her skirts and walked briskly up the hill into the village. Orelia sagged against the pier, quashing the whirl of anxiety threatening to drive her mad. This was the best she could do for now. She was in no shape to try to raise a sword against Remo and the others right now. "I didn't realize she had a daughter," she said to fill the quiet, peering at the siren watching her from over the boat.

"She doesn't anymore," Nerinea said, setting her chin atop her fins. "Not since I was given to the sea."

"Sirens are born the same way as harpies. They are returned by the goddess of the waters they were drowned in," Xellen said quietly.

Orelia's heart ached. "I'm sorry."

Maura returned shortly with paper and ink and Orelia penned out her note. There was so much Orelia wanted to write to her mentor, but when she had written as much as she dared to put into a letter, she gave the woman instructions for the courier.

"I'll do my best," the woman assured her, and produced a small, familiar book from her skirt. "You left this behind last time."

Orelia accepted the small, well-worn book, running her thumb over the familiar fraying along the spine.

Xellen nudged Orelia's shoulder. "What's that?"

A warmth spread along Orelia's cheeks. "Just something I was reading to pass the time."

"Oh, really? Maybe I'll like it." She reached for the book, a teasing smile on her face.

Orelia pressed the green binding into her chest. "It's a tactics book. Part of my training."

"Oh." Xellen dropped her hand, then held out her palm. "I can carry it for you. On the way back." She nodded towards the sea.

The knight stroked the fraying cover again, then swallowed the knot in her throat, and nodded. "Thank you." She flicked her eyes to Maura. "And thank you for saving it for me."

The old woman smiled broadly. "Thank you for trusting me and my Nerinea. Goddesses protect you all."

Chapter Fifteen

Despite the dangers of being spotted this close to shore, Xellen couldn't bear waiting any longer to stretch her wings. Climbing up onto the pier, she launched herself up over the water, beating her wings to climb higher and higher until she caught her first updraft and went spiraling high up into the low clouds. She hung there, suspended between the gods and man, drinking in the pure exhilaration. Flight had been her first real taste of freedom in her life. The first place without bars or locked doors. She could take herself anywhere she wanted to go.

Tucking her wings in close, she dove back down until she could see Orelia carried by the siren as they crossed the water. Ahead of them, the flock was returning to their roost from their early morning hunting. A frisson of excitement sparked through her. She was almost home.

As they grew close, several of the harpies glided down from the top of the roost to a ledge just above the water. Xellen angled her descent to meet them, heart beating so loudly she almost couldn't hear the surf crashing into the rocks below her as she recognized the upturned faces smiling and laughing in relief and welcome.

They welcomed her with open arms, pulling her into embrace after embrace, hands stroking her hair and the feathers on her shoulders, and Xellen sagged into their arms with a grateful sob.

"You've returned," croaked an old, wizened voice from behind the crowd, and the harpies parted for the eldest matron, Savoene. Her feathers were rattled and brittle with years, and she had lost the use of one of her eyes many years ago in a fight to protect the Isle from a raging sea serpent, but her gaze was as steady and stern as the faces carved into the walls high above that watched over them all.

Xellen dropped low to the ground at Savoene's approach, spreading her wings in respect for the matron. The matron's good eye passed over her, and then beyond her, her expression hard and impassive.

"And you have brought us someone."

"A new harpy. She is…an old friend of mine."

Something like a smile cracked the matron's stern expression. "What a rare pleasure. Uaris smiles on you." She turned to the other harpies, their chatter ceasing in an instant. "We must celebrate to welcome another of Uaris' daughters to our flock." A cheer went up, and the matron waited a beat before continuing. "She will need rest. We will make preparations for this evening." She bent close to Xellen, speaking in a hushed tone. "Shall I have her brought to your nest?"

"My—? Oh." Xellen's face flushed a bright, burning red. "Y-Yes."

"Very well." The matron straightened and pointed out two of the harpies. "Bring the sling."

Obediently, the harpies took off from the ledge, swooping low over the water where the siren was just approaching before arcing around and up towards the roost.

With a surge of her body, the siren breached from the water, and the harpies scattered as she landed heavily on the edge of the ledge.

The matron eyed the siren with an undeniable annoyance. "Hello, Nerinea," she said crisply.

The siren grinned toothily, handing Orelia up onto the ledge. "Hello."

Xellen crouched by the knight, gathering her up into her arms. "Just a little bit further," she murmured.

Orelia mumbled something in reply, shivering in Xellen's embrace, and the harpy held her more tightly.

"If that is all, you may go now," Savoene crisply dismissed the siren.

With a laugh that made Xellen's feathers bristle, Nerinea pushed off the ledge and dove into the sea, breaching only once before she disappeared into the depths.

The two harpies Savoene had sent away descended a moment later with a rope dangling between them, a seat of woven canvas and dried seaweed at the center.

With Xellen's help, Orelia climbed into the seat, clinging to the ropes.

"I'll be just behind you," Xellen reassured the knight.

Beating their wings, the harpies slowly took off, kicking up salt spray and rocks as they rose into the air. Xellen followed closely, smiling at the faces peeking out of nests built into the side of the outcrop of rock until, at last, they reached the place she had called home since joining their flock. Flitting beneath the other harpies' wings, she landed on the ledge of her nest and took Orelia's hands, drawing her in through the heavy curtained entrance.

It was dark inside, but warm out of the brisk, sea breeze. It was humble compared to anything Xellen had known in her previous life, but it was hers. Colorful shells, bits of pottery, and colored glass dangled from strings of dried kelp, twisting enchantingly in the breeze from their entrance. She had a few rough pieces of furniture crafted from barrels, crates, and other treasures she and the other harpies had fished from the many shipwrecks littering the rocky coast. Some of the blankets and pillows she had used to make her sleeping nest had been rescued from those same wrecks. Salt-stained and lumpy, but clean after she spent ages washing them to get the salt and smell out, they provided soft and warmth her empty cave otherwise could not.

"You should get out of these wet clothes," she finally said to break the sudden quiet, squeezing Orelia's hands. "I can give you some privacy, if you need. There's a few things in that chest there that you might be able to use if it makes you more comfortable." The knight nodded, shifting uncomfortably, and Xellen smiled reassuringly. "I'll be just outside. No one will come in."

Letting her friend's hands slide from hers, Xellen slipped through the curtain, allowing herself a glance back as the sun fell across Orelia for just a moment. Gods be blessed, but Orelia was as lovely as she remembered. Her golden hair, wet and clinging to her cheeks and neck, gleamed in the sunlight, her new feathers seeming to glow, and where her soaked tunic clung to her, there was an enticing glimpse of the softened curves beneath.

With effort, she pulled her eyes away and stepped out onto the ledge, letting the curtain fall behind her. She'd only just settled down on the warm stone when a harpy she knew well landed on the ledge next to her.

"Florys!" She surged to her feet, throwing her arms around her good friend.

"Welcome back, Xell," her friend mumbled. Florys was smaller than Xellen, but twice as fierce, with a reputation as the flock's most prolific hunter and guard. "I brought you some things to tide you and your *nestmate* over until this evening."

"*Florys.*" Her face was bright red, she could feel it.

"Oh, she denies nothing," Florys observed with a wicked grin.

"We're not... Orelia is my *friend.*"

"Then I still have a chance?" her friend teased, dark brows raised comically high.

Xellen swatted at her arm, and Florys laughed. She held out a basket, woven of dried kelp. There were roasted fish, pickled sea greens, and a salt crusted bottle of wine, along with a jar of grey looking liquid Xellen remembered the foul taste of far too well.

"I'll keep the rest of the flock at bay for now, though I don't know for how long. Everyone is so excited you're back and you've brought a new harpy." Florys glanced past her towards the cave entrance. When she spoke again, her voice lower. "It's lucky. We were going to migrate by the end of this week, but I'm sure the matrons will decide to wait now so we can teach your *friend* to fly."

"The matrons finally came to an agreement?" Xellen asked.

"After it was discovered what happened to you, they decided the risk to the flock if we remained outweighed their concerns over the journey." Florys' smile faded. "I'm sorry we weren't any help. We've been looking every day, but no one knew where you'd been taken."

"It's all right," Xellen soothed her friend, laying her hand over Florys'. "I wouldn't have wanted any of you to get hurt."

"But where did they take you?"

Xellen swallowed. "Lord Boni's menagerie."

Florys' feathers bristled, the glints of red in them glaring in the sun. "Bastard. I wouldn't be sorry to see him and every one of those hunters like him gone."

"Me too," Xellen agreed timidly.

Her friend shook herself, smoothing her feathers down, her smile returning. "Enough unpleasantness. Get some rest and look after your friend so you can join the celebration tonight."

"I will." They exchanged embraces again, and Florys took wing, leaving Xellen by herself on the ledge. She peered into the basket again, picking out a sea green to chew on while she waited, trying not to think about Florys' tease about Orelia. Whatever Xellen's feelings, there was no way she could face the knight after breaking her heart so thoroughly when they said goodbye before.

"I'm dressed."

Xellen turned at the soft voice, smiling at Orelia peeking out through the curtain. "My friend brought us some dinner." She held up the basket. "And some medicine for you."

"Medicine?"

"For the discomfort." She ducked through the curtain, blinking in the dim interior until she could make out the knight. She had dressed in a sleeveless white linen smock that clung to her damp skin, her skin showing pink beneath it, and for the first time, Xellen could appreciate how much Orelia's body had changed and softened to become even more lovely.

"Oh." Orelia ran a hand down her arm, gently picking at a tiny pin. Her arms were covered in light golden-brown downy, the pins of her flight feathers jutting out like banded quills.

"It tastes awful, but it will help." She handed the jar of medicine over and plucked the wine out of the basket. "But Florys brought us this to help wash it down."

Orelia's brows went up. "Where did she get that?"

"We find them in shipwrecks and hidden caches in the caves in our roost." She waggled the bottle. "We'll open it after we eat."

Drawing Orelia into the soft folds of fabric and pillows that made up her nest, she divided out portions of fish and greens for them both, happily enjoying the familiar fare. The knight downed her medicine in a single pull, managing only a tiny grimace, before she accepted the food. Xellen got up after a bit to find something to draw the cork, but when she turned to carry the bottle back to the nest, found Orelia already curled up on her side, eyes barely open.

Smiling fondly, Xellen set the bottle aside and climbed back into the nest, curling up beside Orelia and drawing a blanket over them both. Later then.

"Good night, Orelia," she whispered, pressing her cheek into the knight's shoulder.

Chapter Sixteen

Orelia woke from a dream of golden eyes and soft lips to a particularly sharp cramp between her thighs. She was wet, almost as if she had wet her brais, but there was something else. The strangeness she had been ignoring between her legs was inescapably present. Sweat beaded along her brow, but there was no avoiding it.

Shifting to free her arm of Xellen's sleeping embrace, Orelia bit her lip and reached down her brais between her legs to find a new opening there. It was so wet and sore she thought at first she was bleeding, but her fingers came away covered in clear fluid. She touched herself again, gingerly, feeling over her new anatomy with a growing excitement. Uaris be blessed, but it felt like she had—

Xellen mumbled something behind her, and Orelia quickly jerked her hand out of her brais, wiping her fingers on the stiff fabric. She felt Xellen nuzzle into the back of her neck, her breath hot, and she shuddered, teeth sinking into her lip to choke off her sharp gasp. Gods help her, but something in Orelia thrilled as Xellen's arm tightened around her middle, pulling her closer. Years of tending her own cold bed had left her disinterested in seeking any intimacy, but now, all she wanted was to roll over and enjoy every sweet, torturous thing she had dreamed of.

"Mmh, you all right?"

"Mmhm," Orelia mumbled, swallowing to wet her parched mouth as Xellen shifted against her back with a sigh.

"I suppose we should get washed up. I don't think the matrons would be very happy if we slept through your ceremony." She sat up, leaving behind a strip of cold down Orelia's back where she had lain.

"What does this ceremony involve?" Orelia asked, pushing herself upright, cautious of her tender middle.

"Food and gifts to welcome you to the flock and give everyone a chance to enjoy themselves," Xellen said through a yawn. "If it was earlier in your change, they would help you preen and give you more medicine for any discomfort." She cocked her head mid-stretch. "How *are* you feeling?"

"Better," Orelia said, surprised to find she meant it. Other than the dull soreness between her legs, the rest of her felt significantly better than she had in days.

Xellen smiled. "I'm glad." Shuffling to her feet, she offered Orelia a hand up before she led the way outside.

Orelia squinted against the glare of the late afternoon sun, her eyes streaming painfully. Gods, the sun had never seemed so bright.

A soft, delicate hand took hers and gripped her palm firmly. "Come on, this way."

"Where are we going?" Orelia asked as Xellen drew her down a steep, narrow path that zigzagged along the side of the rock wall.

"The bathing pools."

Orelia followed the gentle tug forward into the blinding sun. She felt much like that wretched heroine in the old tale of the girl held aloft on a bit of wax and cloth, pulled by coy winds up and up to kiss the face of Aaos. An enviable proposition, to kiss a god. But the price for the wind's tricks and the god's caprice had been the girl's mortal life, burned up in an instant like a bit of kindling.

Slowly, the world around Orelia resolved from blinding white into craggy bluffs of rock hung with salt-stained fabrics and ropes. Trees and white bleached branches jut from every available surface, clawing at the blue sky.

Xellen led her up a high path, where some parts were carved out into rough steps. At the heightened vantage, Orelia could see harpies down along the path, some grouped together, some flying above. The monsters Orelia had been taught to fear all her life were now her sisters. While the real monster still lived out there, fearless, brash, and hungry for more death.

Finally, they reached a landing that continued into the side of the cliff. The relief of stepping out of the sun's blinding rays was immediate, but it couldn't prepare Orelia for the charm of the bathing pools. From the back of the cavern, water trickled down along the walls, feeding into several pools, reflecting what sun came in faint dancing ribbons of light along the stone roof.

"It's brighter when the sun is a bit higher," Xellen said. "But your eyes will adjust to the dark."

"I can see just fine," Orelia assured her, blinking the sunspots from her eyes.

Xellen gestured to the pools. "After you, then."

Keeping a hand to the wall, Orelia picked her way down to the edge of the nearest pool, her nails clicking against the stone. The rock was uneven and slick with gathered moisture and pale green algae. Balancing precariously at the edge of the water, she slipped her makeshift shift over her head, letting it drop to the floor in a relatively dry spot.

She shivered, cupping her chest with her palms, marveling again at the swell beneath her hands.

"I'll be nearby if you need help," Xellen said suddenly, the click of her nails trailing towards another pool. "Just let me know."

Orelia frowned. "You aren't coming in with me?"

Xellen froze, her face flushing darkly, and she smiled down at her feet. "I can, I just… thought you might want some privacy."

"You've already seen all of me before," Orelia reminded her, a flush creeping into her own cheeks as she recalled days spent swimming together in the lake between their two estates.

Xellen shifted feet, her nails scraping along the rock. "That was a long time ago."

"It was," Orelia agreed, chewing her lip. "I only thought... Never mind." She shook her head, chasing away the lingering question that had haunted her for so long.

"What is it?" Xellen asked, but Orelia only shook her head again. "Orelia, please."

"It's nothing," the knight insisted, fingering the ties to her brais. "You're right. That was a long time ago. I'm sorry."

"No. *I'm* sorry." Orelia looked up at Xellen, taken off guard by the sadness in her voice. "I've never stopped regretting that day."

"Then why did you leave?" The question came before Orelia could stop it, full of all the hurt and frustration that had never eased in all those years.

Xellen's mouth contorted, her eyes glistening in the faint light. "My...father. He'd promised me to someone without telling me, and then found out about us. His drinking had gotten worse and he..." She bit her lip, the first tears slipping down her cheeks. "He said such terrible things. He meant to hurt you, or worse if I didn't agree to his marriage plan."

Orelia clenched her hands into fists to keep from going to Xellen and comforting her, caught between horror and old pain. "But if you'd come away with me—"

"He was there." Xellen swallowed thickly, her face gone ashen and grey. "He followed me, and when I found him afterwards, he was holding a knife. He meant what he had said."

Orelia rocked back on her heels, too stunned to speak more than a single word. "Why?"

Xellen shook her head. "Debt. My father was a terrible gambler, though mother always took pains to hide it whenever your family visited. She'd hoped to make a match there, but father found someone willing to pay off his debts for a young wife." The harpy shuddered. "He had his own reputation to hide." Her eyes flattened. "There was no accident."

Orelia's heart nearly stopped and her lungs felt crushed as she took in the horrid truths. For not the first time, Orelia wished she could wind back the years and do everything over. She wished she had known—that Xellen had trusted her enough to tell her. That Orelia hadn't failed the one person she had ever loved. "I…I'm sorry."

"Don't be. You didn't—"

"Didn't know? No, but I should have fought for you. We might have—"

"You would have died."

"But you—"

"I am here. Now. With you." Xellen moved, rounding the pool to take Orelia's hands. "I'm sorry I never told you. I was trying to protect you. I thought it didn't matter what happened to me as long as you were all right."

"It matters to me." Xellen looked up at her, eyes wide and glistening and full of vulnerability, and Orelia pulled her into her arms. "You matter to me, and I'm sorry I resented you all these years for that day even as I wished all this time I could have changed your answer."

"I wished I could too," Xellen whispered, clinging tightly to Orelia. "I've done nothing but regret since that day until I saw you again. I thought I was dreaming."

"I thought the same thing when I saw your face," Orelia admitted. "During my fever, I thought you were a spirit to guide my passing, and I—" Her voice cracked, and she struggled to say what had been growing in her since that night when she'd seen Xellen's face through a haze of fevered dreams. "I was glad to see you again."

Xellen's breath hitched, and she peered up at Orelia. "But why? When I…"

"Because…" Orelia sighed, gathering her courage, her heart beating like a caged bird against her ribs. "I've never…loved anyone the way I love you, and the thought of finally being with you again, even in death, made it all worth it."

The words seemed to echo against the stone, over and over, as Xellen stared at her, too stunned to speak. Orelia shifted uncomfortably, the quick fluttering in her chest twisting into sickly unease. She'd said too much. They'd hardly known each other a week after all this time. Xellen probably had someone else by now, someone that was waiting—

Xellen's lips pressed to hers suddenly, the harpy's

arms tightening around her, and Orelia let out a helpless, soft cry before she tilted her head and kissed Xellen with all the desperate passion of five, long years apart. She clutched Xellen to her as if she might drown, as if the world might dissolve back into the smoke of a fever dream if she opened her eyes again. She wished it didn't have to end, and she swayed when Xellen rocked back, breaking the kiss.

"I love you too," the harpy whispered, her cheeks wet and pink as she wept. "I never stopped."

With another breathless sound, Orelia's mouth found Xellen's again, intent on making up for all the time they'd lost.

Chapter Seventeen

Xellen clung to Orelia, her hand sliding up to curl around the back of the knight's neck, tangling in her golden hair as she kissed her deeply, hungrily, possessively. Gods, but she had dreamed of this moment and yet had never imagined what it would truly feel like to have Orelia back in her arms. She wanted... Gods, she wanted.

Grabbing one of Orelia's hands, she guided it to her breast, groaning and biting back a soft curse as the knight's hand cupped around her. Without any hesitation, Orelia stroked her thumb over the hard tip of Xellen's breast, and Xellen arched into the touch.

The knight's mouth strayed from the kiss, and Xellen bit back a needy cry as Orelia's lips brushed down her throat, letting the knight guide her back until she leaned against the cool, stone wall. Fingers never relenting their merciless teasing of one breast, Orelia's mouth skimmed down Xellen's chest and sucked the rigid nub of her other breast into her mouth.

Xellen's mouth fell open in a silent cry, her fingers tightening in the knight's hair, soundlessly urging her on. Orelia sank to one knee before her, suckling and stroking as she let her free hand explore Xellen's belly and hips, then down the backs of her thighs until she reached her knee, urging her feet apart.

"Oh gods," Xellen said, gulping for air as she groped at the wall behind her for support.

Two piercing gold eyes peered up at her, dark with want as Orelia took Xellen's other breast into her mouth, her fingers tracing delicate circles across the sensitive skin just inside her thigh.

Xellen held very still, her breaths shortening, her vision narrowing to Orelia's face, dark and focused in the dim light of the cave. She couldn't feel anything but Orelia's mouth and her fingers stroking lightly across her skin, tracing along her thigh, and then slowly dipped between her legs.

With a cry, Xellen's body arched as Orelia dipped her finger into the wet heat of her, drawing her own wetness to the head of her sex and stroking in slow, languorous swirls. Gods, but it was so much better than the weak pleasure she wrought herself alone at night. Her hips rocked up into the knight's touch, urging her on, hungry for release at Orelia's hand after so long, when the knight pressed her other fingers inside her. She withdrew then slid them back in, keeping time with the endless stroke of her thumb, each thrust sliding higher and deeper, stretching and twisting until Xellen's legs quaked with the effort of keeping upright.

Sweet, blissful release was coming on fast, and she didn't resist its pull, riding the crescendo into a mind-numbing burst of pleasure that threatened to undo her before she finally slumped into Orelia's strength.

"My gods, how do you do that?" she chuckled, her voice coarse.

Orelia smiled coyly. "I listen." She kissed Xellen's breast again, sending another little shock of pleasure through the harpy.

Xellen chuckled, letting her eyes fall on Orelia's bare chest, her breasts standing pert and pink. Her mouth watered. They were such beautiful breasts.

She leaned forward, kissing Orelia's hair and cheek, then her soft parted lips, before tracing lower, kissing a path down the knight's throat.

⬥

Each of Xellen's kisses kindled the fire burning through Orelia that had never gone out, no matter how hard she had tried to quash it. But this was different. They had explored each other before, lying in the sun as they dried from their swim in the cold lake between their estates, giggling and sighing as they kissed and feathered each other with touches. Orelia hadn't let Xellen touch her much, and never below her waist, the stark contrast of what she felt she should be and what Xellen's fingers would find there too sharp a contrast to bear. But now...

She let out a soft whimper as Xellen's lips brushed the hard peak of her newly formed breast, pressing her thighs together at the strange heat sparking between them. It was familiar and yet wholly unlike before. Deeper. A need she didn't quite know how to fill, only that she might go mad without it as Xellen took turns lavishing each of her breasts with gentle suckles.

Without thinking, Orelia reached down between them and cupped herself through her brais, rolling her hips into the heel of her hand, the sensation wringing a gasp from her.

There was a hand at her cheek then, guiding her into a kiss, tongue stroking over hers, and another gentle touch at the back of her hand between her legs, pressing and kneading.

"I want—" Xellen said breathlessly between kisses, "—to do something. For you. Here." She squeezed Orelia's fingers, pressing inwards through her brais.

Orelia's hips jerked into the touch. "Yes," she panted, all anxiety washed away in the tide of feeling Xellen was coaxing from her.

"You're sure?"

The whispered affirmation brought her briefly to her senses, a curl of unease trickling through her middle. "Y–yes, but…" Xellen's eyes found hers, intent and kind. "I've…*changed* down there, and I'm not… It might not be…"

"We don't have to."

"No," Orelia said quickly, stealing a kiss. "No, I want you to. Please. Show me."

Xellen's eyes fluttered closed, and she kissed Orelia again, her touch withdrawing from between Orelia's thighs to tug at the ties to her brais, slowly pulling them down until Orelia felt the cool cave air on her skin.

"Lay back," Xellen instructed, laying a hand in the center of Orelia's chest and pressing her down into the cave floor until she was lying on her back with Xellen over her. She squirmed nervously, heart fluttering in her ribs as Xellen bent her head to trace a line of kisses down her belly, then lower. But she did not keep coyly to her navel or thighs.

"Blessed—!" Orelia's body shot into a rigid arch, her knees clenching around the harpy.

"Is this all right?" Xellen asked, a finger tracing the seam of Orelia's new sex.

No, it was not all right.

It was incredible.

"Gods, yes."

"And this?" Her touch was so gentle, barely skimming over the place where all of Orelia's want had concentrated.

Orelia stifled a cry, biting her lip as she nodded.

"Or…" Xellen's fingers were parting her, and then, just like that, there was a finger inside of her. There was no pain, only a sensation of being penetrated in a way she had never experienced. It was a strange thing for Orelia to contemplate. "Do you want me to stop?"

"No," Orelia rasped. "Don't. Please."

Bending her head, Xellen applied her lips and tongue in tandem with the stroking of her fingers to drive Orelia into madness.

Orelia's blood roared. She was dimly aware of her

fingers clenched in Xellen's dark curls, mindlessly urging her on, a torrent of blasphemy and sharp cries pouring past her lips. She was shaking—trembling—as she rocked her hips to meet every stroke of Xellen's fingers. Something was building inside of her. Not the quick, blinding release she had come to know from her efficient, workman-like self-pleasure she'd engaged in rarely enough. This seemed to simply build and build and build upon itself, coiling tighter and tighter and tighter until—

Xellen's lips closed around the taut bud of her sex and sucked, and something in Orelia broke, wrenching her climax out of her in scorching waves that left her weak, limp, and gasping for breath.

"Xellen," she panted. "Xell…"

"I'm here," Xellen panted, appearing above her to kiss her damp skin. "I have you."

Chapter Eighteen

I will never get anything done again," Orelia declared, hardly able to open her eyes. After a brisk dip in the chilly bathing water, she and Xellen had slipped back to their cozy nest to continue exploring the changes the change had wrought in Orelia's body.

"I'll make sure you won't go hungry," Xellen teased, twisting another pin feather free.

She twitched beneath the harpy, too tired and languid to bother swatting her away. "Promise?"

"Why? Are you hungry?" She pinched another pin feather, twisting it free before she pressed a kiss to the skin beneath.

Orelia cracked an eye at her, mouth curling in a knowing smirk. "I could certainly—"

There was a clatter of nails on stone outside, and the same voice from before called in. "Xellen? You've got half an hour to clean up and be at the meeting place with your nestmate before the matrons send someone meaner to come and get you."

Xellen groaned, smiling as she looked over her shoulder at the curtained entrance. "We'll be there."

"You better." There was another scrape of nails and the sound of wing beats, and they were alone again.

"Do we have to?" Orelia murmured as Xellen drew away from her.

"We do." She offered Orelia her hand and drew her up with her. "Come on. We should wash up again."

"Oh, just let me rot," Orelia groaned. "The power of flight, but not a flint amongst your whole flock?"

"Sometimes in winter. It can be dangerous to gather wood from the mainland."

It was a sharp reminder of what sort of life Orelia had before, and where she stood now. It didn't feel so different after years of being tormented by Remo and other men like him.

There was a touch at her cheek, drawing her back to Xellen. "Don't make that face," Xellen murmured, stroking her thumb along the soft down speckling her cheek.

"It just feels surreal to be here." She touched Xellen's hand, careful not to scratch her with her new sharpened nails that had come in. "I'm glad it's with you."

A soft rose color flushed Xellen's cheeks, and she leaned forward to press a kiss to Orelia's lips. "I'm happy you're here too."

They freshened with rags and clean water from a large, pink half-shell perched atop a barnacle scarred barrel, and Xellen waited patiently while Orelia slipped into her borrowed smock. It was strange and wonderful to freely wear a dress and see her new body underneath, and she couldn't stop running her hands down her chest and along her hips, twisting left and right to watch the skirt swirl around her legs.

"You look beautiful," Xellen murmured, taking Orelia's hand to lead her out onto a narrow path along the cliffside. She moved slowly, the trek all the more difficult in the waning sunlight of the day, her new feet still clumsy along the jagged rock.

As they wound higher, Orelia began to make out a sound above the crashing surf that slowly resolved into the low percussive beat of a drum. A lub-dub that seemed to match the beating of her heart. The sound grew louder, beating faster and faster until, suddenly, the path crested the top of a ledge.

Below them, the other harpies had gathered at the sunken center of their outcrop, surrounded by colorful streams of fabric, and at the very center was a pile of grey, gnarled driftwood left to dry and crack in the sun.

The knight swallowed, anxious to find herself the center of a ceremony she knew nothing about, when Savoene stepped forward.

"Praise to Uaris! We welcome our new fledgling!"

Someone struck a flint and sent the pile of wood up in a roar of flame that sent a round of wild caws and hoots through the gathered flock.

"Come," the old harpy said, beckoning for Orelia to descend the steps cut into the stone. "We will celebrate the goddess' blessing of life and sisterhood. Her love is the wind beneath our wings."

The fire surged and licked the air, sending golden embers sparking into purple twilight, and for a moment, Orelia thought she could almost make out the golden eyed face she'd dreamt of in her fever.

Fingers squeezed hers, and Orelia looked back at Xellen, her heart falling out of sync with the drums below as it thudded against her ribs. "I'll be right behind you," Xellen whispered.

Turning back to the old matron, Orelia squared her shoulders and seized her courage. This was like any other ceremony or event a knight was expected to attend.

She descended the stairs, the beat of the drums growing not louder, but more insistent until she could feel the pulse in her head, her chest, even her blood.

Savoene held up a hand as she drew near, and Orelia stopped, swaying in time with the drums. "Give us your name, fledgling. Not the one that has died, but the one you have been reborn into."

"Orelia."

The matron spread her wings, fire shining through the tattered feathers like golden stars. "Orelia." There came a murmur from the ring of harpies, a rolling echo of her name washing in like the tide. "Tonight, we will celebrate your new birth, and tomorrow, teach you how to leave the nest." Stepping forward, Savoene took both of Orelia's hands in hers, drawing her close. "We hope you will nest here for many more years. Welcome to our flock, Orelia."

Cheers went up around them, the drums pounding as Savoene slipped her hands from Orelia's and the crush of the flock descended upon her. Arms looped around her in embrace, and trinkets were hung around her neck and pressed into her hands as she was towed this way and that through a sea of excited voices to meet the harpies that claimed her to be their sister.

The rest of the night brought back a dizzying whirl of childhood memories for Orelia that she hadn't thought of in ages. She had only ever attended a handful of balls, and her family had only ever thrown a few small affairs at their country home. Colorful dresses, decadent food, and streams of wine as the night passed in a swirl of dancing and gossip.

The harpies had somehow managed to throw a celebration fit for a princess. Fish, beef, and even pork was all prepared in a wide variety of ways with olives, capers, berries, grape leaves, and herbs. Bottles of wine and even a cask of sweet cider flowed freely into wooden cups pressed one after the other into Orelia's hands, which she eagerly downed. She twisted in place every chance she got, trying to catch a glimpse of where Xellen might have gone, but couldn't make her out from the shadows and feathers.

Instruments appeared from seemingly nowhere to join the beating drums, and before she knew it, Orelia was drawn into a wild, spinning dance with partner after partner before she found herself pulled away by Xellen into a discreet corner.

"Here," she whispered, producing a crown of white and yellow wildflowers.

Orelia's eye lit up. "You remembered?"

"Of course." She set the crown on Orelia's brow. "I practiced as often as I could after you taught me how to make them."

Orelia touched one of the silky petals, running the pad of her finger down it. "Where did you find them?"

"I may have had some help," Xellen said evasively, catching Orelia's hand and pressing a kiss to her knuckles. "Everyone's excited you're here. I can't wait until you can meet them all properly."

A family that wanted her just as she came. "I look forward to it," Orelia murmured.

"There you are!" Florys came marching around the hidden nook, brows high in amusement. Dressed only in a richly dyed fabric tied loosely about her hips, her dark hair coiled into a pile on top of her head held in place pins decorated with glittering bits of sea glass, Florys was the picture of elegant beauty.

Orelia stared, at once taken aback and enthralled by the harpy's boldness. The knight could only dream of appearing so effortlessly beautiful.

Florys laughed, her feathers ruffling in delight. "If Xell hadn't already taken you to roost, I certainly would have after *that* look." She gestured with her chin back towards the fire. "Come on. It's time for the next part."

"Next part?" Orelia stammered, shaking herself from her stupor.

"Of the ceremony," Xellen filled in, her fingers

squeezing Orelia's.

Curious, though not entirely free of a curl of anxiety low in her belly, Orelia followed Florys, Xellen close at her side. The harpy led her back to the fire where Savoene and several other older harpies had gathered around a soft looking pallet of blankets and furs.

"Sit," the matron instructed, kneeling at the edge of the pallet.

Orelia did as she was instructed, and someone pressed a cup of warmed wine into her hands, the smell of spices tickling her nose as they lifted her hands, tipping the cup against her lips. It went down smoothly, settling in her belly with more warmth than any of the other wines she'd tasted that evening.

Another harpy touched her arm, and she nearly jumped out of her skin, drink sloshing over her fingers.

"Uaris gave you breath, but it is not an easy rebirth," Savoene said calmly, refilling her cup and pressing it to Orelia's mouth again. "Tonight, we ease your passage into our world and welcome you to our family."

There was another touch at her shoulder, and Orelia twitched at the slick sensation of oil against skin and feathers.

"It's all right," Xellen's voice murmured in her ear, warm and sweet with drink. "It's to ease the itching and help your feathers grow in."

Orelia nodded, her head heavy and the cup in her hands sloshed again before hands helped press it to her lips again. She drank until the cup was empty and it was filled again. Savoene was speaking, but the words slipped past Orelia like a stream over rocks, low and growling. Or maybe she was singing.

Orelia swayed to the sound, her eyes closing, thoughts sinking into syrupy contentment as a pair of arms looped around her waist. She sank back into warmth and softness, curling into the familiar sea spray scent of Xellen, nuzzling her face into the downy softness of her neck. Whatever was happening, if Xellen was there with her, everything would be all right.

Chapter Nineteen

Days became a week, a week became another, but no matter how peaceful or brilliant her time with the flock and with Xellen was, Orelia couldn't help but watch the horizon for smoke. There had been no return letter, to her knowledge, no sighting of an army marching in or out of the Boni estate, no unusual stirrings in the village that she could see. Convincing lords, gathering troops, and marching an army took time. But Orelia couldn't help a niggling worry that the letter had never made it to her mentor, or had been cast aside—that an army of mercenaries and traitorous knights was about to march on the Crown's territory.

She wished she could put eyes on the lord's estate herself to see how close they were to marching, but despite days of practice, her wings still weren't strong enough.

That first step out into thin air had been exhilarating and terrifying as she found herself lofted by the capricious wind beneath her new feathers. Then came the climb back up. Even with Xellen and her friend's help, Orelia couldn't keep at the practice long before she collapsed in exhaustion, her back, chest, and shoulders burning. She hadn't been so sore since first learning the sword.

After a couple days, Xellen had been called back to her duties in the flock, flying out before the first crack of dawn and just after the last glimpse of sunset to hunt fish for meals, which they cooked amongst the hot ash and coals of banked fires. It was plain fare, even with strips of seaweed to pick up the bits of baked fish with, but it was miles better than the raw rabbit the Lord Boni and Remo had seen fit to give her and Xellen.

Orelia stretched her wings in the silvery light of the half-moon, craning her head, but there was no sight of the hunting party yet. So, she leapt out into the air.

Salt air rushed to fill the curve of her wings, slowing her descent. She tucked her legs close, the way Xellen had shown her, and banked to one side, arching clumsily around the outcropping to the ledge she had first arrived at.

Her landings were as graceful as her flights, and even though she cupped her wings and arched back the way she'd seen the other harpies do every day, she still landed too quickly. Her claws caught in the rough rocks, and she went tumbling head over heels into a sprawl. As if to add insult to injury, a spray of frigid sea water splashed over the ledge, soaking her makeshift dress and drenching her hair.

There was a peal of musical laughter, and Orelia glared at the dark eyed siren peeping over the ledge, enormous claws dug into the stone. "I've been watching you. You're not a very graceful bird."

"I haven't been one long," Orelia huffed, wringing out her dress.

Nerinea grinned, showing all of her long, dagger-like teeth. "I see you looking down the cliffs every day. You're worried about those men that chased you."

"Of course, I am." Orelia flung her dress down, nails tapping impatiently against the stones. "You haven't seen anything, have you?"

The siren tilted her head one way and then the other. "I might. I can."

"So, you haven't."

"But I can." Nerinea's body slithered upwards onto the rocks until she towered over Orelia. "You share your supper with me, and I will keep watch over your men."

Orelia fought the urge to shrink back from under the shadow of the siren, grasping at the thin hope Nerinea's words offer. "You'll tell me if they start to gather forces or march out of their estate if I share fish with you?"

"Yes." The siren's eyes seemed to stretch in excitement, deep black pools that betrayed her hunger. "Leave it here on this ledge, and I will tell you if your men act."

Orelia glanced up the sheer cliff at her back, guilt worming through her belly, but she didn't know of any other way to know if soldiers marched for the capital or the village. "All right. I'll do it."

"Wonderful. I'll see you later." With a surge of her tail, Nerinea rolled back into the waves and disappeared into the sea, leaving Orelia uncertain if she had just made a huge mistake.

Chapter Twenty

Another week flew by in a flurry of activity. Still not strong enough to hunt, Orelia volunteered to learn other tasks from the harpies that stayed behind during the hunts. There was cleaning and drying foods, braiding rope, weaving baskets, and a hundred other intricate, vital skills to learn. Of all of them, Orelia found she enjoyed making rope the most, the intricate, repetitive patterns soothingly distracting from her anxiety over what news the siren would bring her that evening.

She tried to listen to the gossip amongst the other harpies, make out what sorts of things were happening amongst the flock. She caught bits here and there—trouble with nestmates, boasts and brags, aching joints—but found the quick back and forth of names she wasn't familiar with impenetrable.

One thing that was hard to miss, however, was the looming migration the flock had planned. Orelia's arrival had delayed the flock leaving, but there was talk of a new plan. Half of them would stay, continue to live as they had here on the outcrop, while the rest flew ahead to make ready their new home. When everything was ready and safe, they would send messengers back to guide the rest of the flock to them.

Orelia eyed the heavy clouds above that had been gathering all day, rolling in from the horizon in a dark line. It looked to be a nasty one, the sea below whipped to a grey froth by the steadily increasing winds. Stretching her wings, she determined to get in a quick practice before the weather turned, when she spied a sleek, dark shape slipping through the water towards the ledge she always flew to.

The knight's heart thudded against her ribs. The siren. She was early.

Leaning out over the ledge, Orelia tipped into the air and fell.

Her stomach floated up into her throat, eyes watering as the salt wind whipped at her face and hair, the world flying past until, at the last possible moment she dared, she snapped out her wings. Her shoulders burned as she arced just above the water, toes skimming the waves. She beamed, heart racing with the sheer thrill of it. Never had she imagined she might catch the eye of a goddess and earn a blessing as wonderful as this. It was a gift she could never repay, even if she tried for the rest of her life.

With a few powerful surges of her wings, she rose until she was just above the height of the ledge, then leaned back, letting her wings catch the air and slow her until, with another few flaps to keep her balance, she landed on the stone, nails gripping the crevices.

Behind her, there was a loud splash, and Nerinea joined her on the ledge, pointed teeth showing in a wide grin. "You've gotten better," she remarked, the lilting song of her voice high with excitement. "I hope you've gotten stronger too."

"What have you seen?"

Nerinea flicked her tongue between her teeth, eyes glittering with excitement. "Ships carrying men and weapons from across the sea. They hide out on the sea and sneak onto land at night in their little boats."

The mercenaries. The blood drained from Orelia's face. If they were gathering in force, they must be planning to march soon without any anticipation of resistance. There was no more time to wait and see if her letter made it to the capital. If she didn't do something, they would take the countryside by force. They would start a war.

⬥ ⬥ ⬥

Despite living and sleeping together, Xellen felt she had seen Orelia less and less during their stay with the flock. Not because they never saw one another, but because Orelia was constantly somewhere else, even when she was curled up in Xellen's arms. Xellen tried not to pry. A lot had happened in a short amount of time, and Xellen knew well what it was like to have one's life turned upside down, even if it was for the better. But tonight, the distance hung between them like an impenetrable fog, thick and cold and grey, and no matter how Xellen wrapped her arms around Orelia, she couldn't help but feel like she was slipping away.

"What's wrong?"

Orelia shifted restlessly in her arms, her gaze fixed on the curtain, thunder rumbling threateningly beyond. "I'm not—"

"Lia," Xellen warned, pushing up onto her elbow so she could look Orelia in the face. "Don't try to put me off. Whatever it is, I want to know."

The knight shifted again, frowning before she would meet Xellen's gaze. "Ships arrived at the lord's estate. I think they are going to move out soon."

"But your mentor should be on his way, right? He would have gotten your letter by now."

"If it made it. If I were Remo, I would have guards posted to stop any outgoing mail from the village to make certain no one could warn His Majesty of what is happening here."

A knot twisted itself in Xellen's gut. "You're not thinking of going back there, are you? You're just one person. What are you going to do if they capture you again? Or worse?"

"And what am I going to do if I don't at least try? I couldn't live with myself knowing I did nothing to stop them."

"And I couldn't live if you didn't come back." Xellen cupped Orelia's cheek, stroking her thumb over the arch of her cheekbone. She wished she knew what to say to change Orelia's mind and convince her to stay, to come with the flock and leave all of this behind. She wished she was enough. "Please."

Orelia closed her eyes and Xellen knew she had lost. She withdrew her hand, shrinking back when Orelia reached for her.

"Xell…" Orelia said softly, but Xellen shook her head, fighting the tears threatening to fall.

"Go," she said, fixing her glare on the wall. "Just go." She saw Orelia's lips part to say something more, but then she sighed and, getting to her feet, ducked through the curtain.

Xellen waited, wishing and hoping beyond hope that Orelia would come back through the curtain again, but she was alone. Again.

"Uaris, why?" she sobbed, pulling her knees up to her chest.

Chapter Twenty-One

Not for the first time, Orelia wished things could be different. In any other life, she would be back there, in Xellen's nest, or sharing their marriage bed at their country estate. Instead, she was perched on a rock soaked in salt spray from the waves churned up by the approaching storm.

Of course, it hadn't been her choice to take this path five years ago. She had taken a knee and all but begged Xellen to marry her to come away to live out the rest of their lives like those warm summer days in the country together. But Xellen had turned her down—out of fear for both of their lives—and accepted a short, miserable life spent with a man who had caused her end.

And Orelia, with nowhere left to turn, had taken up the mantle of knight to protect her family from ruin and herself from utter destitution. How funny the gods had seen fit to reunite them only for Orelia to turn down the prospect of all the love and comfort she had been wanting for duty and honor. But what else could she do?

Lightning streaked across the sky, painting the frothing water a bright, luminous white for just a moment as the gathering storm threatened to break at any moment. She hoped the siren saw her and knew to come. The plan she was quickly putting together wouldn't work without her help.

She waited, crouching down on the ledge as the wind began to rise, threatening to tear her off the rock with its stiffest gusts when in a surge of frigid water, Nerinea appeared on the ledge beside her.

"I don't have any news," the siren said, her voice barely audible over the storm.

"I need your help," Orelia shouted over the din as thunder rolled over them in a deafening rumble.

"Oh?" Nerinea's eyes glinted in the flash of lightning.

"I need you to take me to your mother again."

The siren leaned towards her. "Why?"

"I need to ask her for something. And then I need you to take me out to the ships. I can't fly the distance yet, especially in this storm."

Sharp, shark's teeth glinted against the siren's dark skin. "What *are* you planning?"

She described in brief what her plan was, and Nerinea let out a laugh like a clap of thunder. "Oh, I like this plan. Come, while the tide is with us."

With a last glance back at the entrance she knew was somewhere out of sight above her, Orelia whispered a prayer. "Blessed Uaris, keep her safe." Then, taking the siren's outstretched hand, she let Nerinea pull her into the restless depths.

It was cold—shockingly so, the tides and currents pushing and pulling against Orelia even as Nerinea pulled her into her arms and up onto her back, guiding her grip around her neck. "Hold tight," the siren said, voice clear as bells even under water. "And keep your head up."

Orelia struggled to do as she was told, her arms burning, lungs half full of water as the stormy waves caught her by surprise, slapping her cheeks until they stung. It was a mercy the inlet the old woman lived on was not far. By the time Nerinea helped drag her onto the shore beneath the rickety pier, Orelia was heaving up mouthfuls of water.

She knelt in the rocks and sand, coughing and sputtering, shivering as the wind whipped around her. But there was no time to waste. She needed the cover of darkness for her plan to work, and there was still the journey to the estate to make.

Staggering to her feet, she followed the muddy path up to the hut she had become so familiar with during her stay and knocked on the door. She waited, hoping Maura would answer a strange knock at night, but it was impossible to hear anything inside over the howling wind and thunder. She knocked again, pressing her ear to the door, when it suddenly flew open and Orelia found a fishing spear pointed directly beneath her chin.

"What d'you—Oh, dear. My apologies." The woman swung the spear away, and Orelia let out a relieved breath. "Come in. Come get yourself dry." She ushered Orelia, stationing her by the hearth. "Now what're you doin' here out in weather like this at this time of night?"

Orelia eased closer to the fire, sighing in relief even as she shivered. "I-I need to ask another favor. Please."

"If it's another letter, I'm happy to—"

"It's too late for that," Orelia said, voice heavy with dread. " I can't wait any longer for an answer. The lord's forces are gathering. There are ships of mercenaries out there, and they are getting ready to march."

The woman frowned, eyes narrowing in thought. "You don't say? Is this what that letter was about?"

"Yes, but I'm afraid whatever may come of it will come too late."

Her frown deepened, furrows trenching her forehead and cheeks. "So what's this plan of yours?"

Taking a deep breath, Orelia described her intentions, and Maura let out a bark of laughter nearly identical to her daughter's. She knelt next to Orelia and opened a dusty box by the hearth, retrieving something small and wrapping it in a cloth with string.

"You'll be needin' this then. I'll give it to you on one condition." Maura waited, holding Orelia's gaze firmly until the knight inclined her head. "My son and most of the youngins in our village were summoned by the lord to his estate. Whatever your plan, I beg you to send him and the others home to us. They didn't… They weren't given no choice. And I can't…" She looked towards the door—towards the sea—and Orelia knew what she couldn't say.

"My target is the knight commander and mercenaries," she swore. "If I know Remo, he'll have them camping out on the estate's lawn rather than within the manse. If everything goes all right, they should be able to flee in the chaos."

The woman clutched the bound package to her chest, eyes glittering with tears, then nodded. "Here." She pressed the cloth into Orelia's hands. "Go stop those dogs. Send our boys back to us."

"I will," Orelia promised, slipping her fingers over the old woman's hands. "Thank you."

"No. Thank you. I know life hasn't been kind for you to wind up standin' here like this, and for you to still… My Nerinea…" A watery smile flickered across the woman's face. "Bless you. And bless my poor Nerinea. She deserved so much better than I could give her. Goddess protect you both."

"Goddess, protect us all," Orelia murmured.

Chapter Twenty-Two

Rain fell in dark sheets beyond Xellen's curtains, almost hard enough to drown the sound of the raging surf throwing itself against the rocks below. There was no sign of Orelia, no matter how much Xellen prayed and hoped. The knight wasn't coming back.

Her eyes prickled with tears, and she squeezed them shut, vainly trying to hold them in—to hold everything in. She let the curtain fall and dropped back into her nest, curling into a tight ball. How had everything gone so wrong again? How did it hurt this much after she'd already left Orelia before?

"Damn the gods," she whimpered as her tears overflowed and ran down her stinging cheeks again. "Damn Uaris." She rolled over, putting her back to the curtain Orelia had disappeared out of and covering herself with her wings.

But rather than the soft comfort of her familiar nest, all she could think of was how very empty it felt. She wriggled deeper, determined not to think on it, when something dug into her ribs.

Fury lit through her in an instant, and she snatched the thing up and reared back to fling the thing away, only to realize it wasn't an errant rock or stick. It was a book.

Frowning, she crawled to a bowl near her nest, jostling the water within. A soft, blue glow from the tiny creatures within illuminated the stones, and she tipped the book towards it to read what it was.

There was no title, no author, nothing at all on the outside to denote what it was. Only a tattered, stained green binding. Opening it, she was surprised when several dried flowers fell out from between the pages, which turned out to be filled with not just printed poetry, but little handwritten annotations in the margins. Some were simply amusing remarks on the contents of the poems. A few were quotes from other poets, philosophers, and crude workmen. But then, there were the other pieces. Little remarks comparing descriptions in the poems to someone, notes on what this someone would and wouldn't like, and even fragments of poems by the mysterious annotator about them. And then, on the last page, a dedication, penned in next to an ancient dried golden teardrop.

To my love. May my words reach you on that final beach and bring you the comfort and peace I never could in life. I am yours unto the day we meet again upon those sands.

Xellen turned the book over in her hands, running her thumb over the rough cover as her eyes brimmed over at the signature below the dedication. "Damn you."

Orelia

"I can't… I can't. I can't, I'm sorry," she whimpered, clutching the hard edges of the book in her shaking fingers, her heart squeezing in her chest. It was too dangerous. They'd both be killed, or captured.

But if she stayed here, her heart would die. Alone.

Pressing the book to her lips, she set it down in the center of the nest, hands shaking as she got to her feet, and stepped out into the storm.

⫷⫸

The sea was shockingly cold. Every inch of Orelia had gone numb by the time Nerinea slowed in the water, her body dipping to vertical.

"We're close," the siren whispered just loud enough to be heard over the storm's wrath.

Squinting through the salt spray and rain, Orelia could just barely make out the shadowy shapes of ships ahead of them. Three, just as Nerinea had reported. There were no lights aboard. It was like looking at ghosts. They had chosen their night of approach well. No one from shore would see a single thing

She wrenched her teeth open, managing an affirmative through her chattering and shivering before another storm whipped wave rolled over her head.

The siren slid smoothly forward through the water to the nearest ship, grasping the hull with her wickedly curved claws. "Put your legs around me."

Orelia struggled to move her numb, leaden legs, but somehow managed to get them around Nerinea's waist, gripping as best she could.

"Now hold tight."

Orelia made out a glint of sharp, white teeth before Nerinea surged upwards, body undulating. The knight let out an involuntary yelp and clasped the siren's neck more tightly as the siren caught the edge of the deck and hauled herself up. Grasping Orelia by her shoulder, Nerinea dragged the knight off her back and onto the deck.

Orelia lay there a moment, shivering violently in the night air, her arms and legs stiff and numb. Slowly she forced her body to unclench, pushing her hair out of her eyes as she rolled to her hands and knees and coughed up a good quantity of sea water. "Oh gods," she rasped.

The deck was empty, any sailors left aboard sheltering below decks from the storm's wrath. Glancing back, she found Nerinea had disappeared back into the water. She was on her own.

Lifting her hand, she reaffirmed the pouch she had tied to her wrist remained and dragged herself to her feet. She stumbled on numb, clumsy feet to the door that led below decks. She hesitated, pressing her ear to the door, but she couldn't hear anything over the storm.

She tried the latch, pleased when it came easily, and, setting a shoulder to the wood, shoved it closed behind her. Darkness more complete than even the stormy night outside closed in around her. She waited for her eyes to adjust, but there was nothing to adjust to. Reaching out, she felt for the wall then eased one foot forward until she found the edge of a stair. She cautiously picked her way down, one feeling step after another, until she reached the floor, keeping her head ducked beneath the low press of the ceiling.

She'd never been aboard a ship before, but she had an idea of what she was looking. She felt her way down the blackened hall until she heard the tell-tale rattle of a hatch underfoot. Bending, she hooked her fingers in the lattice of wood and hauled, lifting the door on its hinges, and slipping down the stair into the belly of the ship.

Stale, stinking water pooled around her toes when she stepped off the last stair. Wrinkling her nose, she did her best not to breathe in the rank smell as she hunched over, reaching blindly into the dark. Her hand bumped something solid, and she briefly felt along it, grinning when she realized the shape of it.

Using her new claws that had replaced her once dull fingernails, she scratched an indentation into the surface, brushing the shavings in a little pile. Then, fishing out her borrowed tools from the pouch on her wrist, she struck them over the little pile.

It took a few tries, but eventually, she managed to make her shaking hands work, and sparks leapt from the flint and iron. For a split second, she caught a glimpse of the barrel she had clawed and her little pile of shaving, and she adjusted her hands. A few more hard strikes, and an ember caught. She quickly scratched out more wood, feeding the little spark of fire, breathing life into it until a tiny tongue of flame licked up from the wood.

Looking around, she found a crate nearby and, wedging her claws under part of it, she managed to splinter off a bigger chunk. Picking a precious piece of fatwood from within the pouch, she jammed it into the end of the stick, and stuck it into the tiny flame.

Orange light leapt into the frayed bits of wood on the end of the stick, kindling the fat wood into a brightly glowing ember, and she held it aloft as she waded through the ship's hold. She scratched little piles of kindling into the lids of any wooden container she found, touching her ember to them each in turn and coaxing them to ignite, but they struggled to stay burning.

But then, nestled carefully between other boxes and lashed together, she found a selection of clay jars. Tall enough to reach her knee and unadorned but for the wax sealing the top, she couldn't make out what they might contain. Alcohol, with luck. She peeled the wax back and peered inside, surprised by the smell of tallow. She opened the others, equally baffled to find that while some of them also contained fat, some were filled with sticky resin, or a grey powder.

Sticking her hand into the jar of resin, she smeared the sticky substance over the nearest barrel and touched her ember to it. The spark smoldered for a moment, then burst into flame that licked across the barrel.

Orelia's lips pulled back in a vicious smile, and she

thrust her hand into the resin again.

Wood crashed against wood behind her, and Orelia whipped around to find a man in sailor's dress, face red with drink beyond the bristle of his black beard and eyes wide as he stared at her.

"Fu—"

He stammered something in a language she didn't know, the mug in his hand clattering as it struck the steps.

She ran for him, not certain what she would do with only her bare hands, but she couldn't let him—

"Help!" he bellowed, shoving the hatch up. "Monster! Monster!"

Swearing darkly, Orelia snatched at the man's ankle, her nails cutting into the flesh as she yanked. He went down with a cry, his head bouncing off the top stair with an ugly crack before the hatch slammed shut on his arm. Orelia could hear the bone snap beneath his scream. If his shipmates hadn't heard him before, they definitely had now.

Letting the man go, she spun to the rest of the hold, taking in the small fires struggling to catch and burn in the damp. It wasn't nearly the destruction she had hoped to cause. She glanced back at the sailor whimpering on the stair. She had a few more seconds at best before someone else showed up. She should make the best of it. Crossing the hold, she planted one foot and kicked the jar of resin.

It cracked near in half at the top, shards from the brittle edge flying off. She stamped on it again, smashing the pot open, resin oozing out across the boards. Then, she snatched up pieces of the jar, scooping up globs of resin, and holding them to the fire burning energetically through the barrel next to her, and flung them to the far parts of the hold. Fire splattered across the wood, heat and smoke rapidly building in the tight space, stinging her eyes, nose, and lungs. It was time to go.

Climbing past the whimpering sailor, Orelia shoved the hatch up only to narrowly miss the toe of a boot aimed at her nose. She ducked, pulling the hatch down with her, and made a grab for the man's ankle, but he leapt out of reach.

"All hands!" he bellowed, backing down the hall. "To arms! All han—"

Throwing the hatch open, Orelia rushed him, barrelling down the hall with arms wide, feathers bristling of their own accord. The man let out a scream and turned to flee, colliding with another sailor who had just emerged from further down the hall to come see what all the ruckus was, and they went down in a heap. Orelia leapt over them, swinging around the stairs to make her escape on deck, when the door at the top opened.

There was a glint of steel, and Orelia threw herself backwards just in time to evade the man's sword. She ducked his next swing then lunged up the stair, driving her shoulder into his gut. Scrambling over him, she reached for his sword hand when her head jerked back with a sharp, burning pain. She screamed as he wrenched her back by her hair, cursing her in his mother tongue as he raised his sword.

"No!" Bracing with one hand, she clawed at his hand in her hair with the other, her nails peeling ribbons of skin away.

The sword clattered from his grip and he shrieked, tossing her down the stairs to cradle his hand. She caught herself at the bottom, the world whirling around her as she staggered back to her feet, stumbling unsteadily back upwards. Blood ran like water through the man's fingers, pooling on the stairs, and he did nothing but stare at his ruined hand as Orelia ran past.

Outside, waves curled over the edge of the deck, spilling frigid sea water over the boards. Orange light glittered off the water and it took Orelia a moment to realize it was her fire. Some of it must have reached outside the hold.

Grinning fiercely, she grasped the edge of the deck and threw herself into the air. The shock of the water was instant and fierce, stealing her breath. She hung in the rolling grasp of the waves, pulled and pushed and spun, her chest aching and her limbs numb, when a dark shape swept her up in its embrace.

Her head breached the surface, and she greedily gulped down air.

"You're bleeding," Nerinea murmured, her breath a cold wind at Orelia's ear.

"Ran into trouble," Orelia said between gasps, lifting her chin above a cresting wave. She looked back at the ship, watching with satisfaction as orange flames licked up the belly of the ship. Even if the other two got away, if she managed to scuttle that one, there would be no way to deny the ship's presence to any Crown authority, which any respecting lord would have reported immediately. That was one strike against Lord Boni. Now for the next blow. "Take me to shore. I need to get to the estate now."

The siren's body rippled as she changed directions in the water, cutting across the waves. "As you wish. I think I will entertain myself with these sailors while you climb. I do hope they decide to jump."

⊰⊱⊰⊱⊰

Xellen followed the curving edge of the coastline as it rose sharply above the sea. The wind was easier to bear close to the sheltering cliffs, but it was impossible to see how far she had come through the fog and pelting rain. That was until a ghostly glow illuminated the mist, red and flickering. She banked towards it, her stomach coiling in knots as the dreadful shape of a ship engulfed in flames loomed suddenly out of the storm.

There was a horrible scream, and she watched as a tiny boat in the water capsized, and a dark sinuous tail breached before one of the men disappeared beneath the waves.

Nerinea. If she was here, then…

Xellen turned to shore, letting the storm lift her until she reached the top of the cliff once more. She perched on a peak of rock, nails gripping tightly as she leaned out to peer down the cliff face, but the fog was as impenetrable as before.

"Orelia!" She strained her ears, but no sooner had she called the knight's name, the storm tore her voice from her lips and vanished it into the rain and wind. She called again, hoping and praying she hadn't missed her, that Orelia hadn't gone ahead to the estate already without her while Xellen wept pathetically in her nest and let her slip away again. "Orelia!"

"Xellen?"

Xellen's heart leapt into her throat, and she scrambled forward to find a pale hand reaching over the ledge to grip the craggy rock with newly grown claws. "Orelia!" She grabbed the woman's hand, pulling as Orelia scrambled over the ledge, and snatched her up in a tight embrace.

"What are you doing here?" Orelia asked through chattering teeth, her arms trembling as they slipped around Xellen's back.

"I couldn't let you go. Not again." She squeezed Orelia tight, shivering as frigid water ran down between them. She leaned back and took in the sopping rag the knight still wore modestly, sodden with sea and rain water. "We've got to get you out of that." She reached for the knot under Orelia's chest, and the knight shied away.

"What?"

"You're freezing. We've got to get you dry."

"It's raining."

"Your feathers will shed the rain. This—" She tugged at the scrap of fabric again. "—will hold it."

Orelia seemed to shrink in on herself, worrying her lip. It was a look Xellen knew too well from the few times she and Orelia had shared more than time by the lake.

"It's all right," she reassured her, touching her arm.

The knight was silent, her golden eyes wide and nervous, before she nodded. With trembling hands, Orelia fumbled the waterlogged knot until it finally tore free and the sodden fabric fell away. She folded her arms over her chest, hiding the pale shapes of her breasts, and shuddered.

Xellen eased closer, pressing against Orelia's side and lifting a wing over the knight's head to shield her from the rain. "We should get you someplace dry."

"I'll be fine," Orelia said, pushing away and getting to her feet. "You should go back."

"No. Lia—" Xellen caught the knight's hand, pulling her back around to face her. She wanted to ask Orelia to come away with her, to go back to their warm nest and forget this vengeance of hers, but the words wouldn't come. They would make it through this together, or not at all. Taking a deep breath, she screwed up her courage, and forged ahead. "What's your plan?"

Orelia's eyes widened with surprise before she seemed to master herself. "Dangerous," she said tersely.

"All the more reason not to let you go alone." Raising onto her toes, Xellen slipped her arms behind Orelia's neck, pressing against her. "I won't lose you again."

The knight's eyes slipped closed as she gathered

Xellen against her. "I can't let you get hurt because of me."

"They hurt me too," she said gently. Orelia flushed, glancing away, and Xellen cupped her cheek, drawing her back. "We do this together. Then, when we go back to the flock, we never look back."

Orelia's gaze softened with unshed tears, and her arms tightened around the harpy. "You're sure?"

A smile curved Xellen's mouth. "Never more." With a tug, she pulled Orelia down into a kiss, letting it say everything she couldn't put into words—that she would rather face whatever end might come with Orelia than continue living without her.

"I love you," she whispered against the knight's mouth.

"I love you, too," Orelia murmured, fingers winding in Xellen's black curls. "We should—"

"Yes. We should." With a faint sigh of regret, Xellen stepped back, letting her hands trace down the knight's arms. "So, what is this plan of yours?"

Orelia nodded towards the looming forest, the spaces between the trunks full of mist and night. "We're going to burn that menagerie to the ground."

Chapter Twenty-Three

Xellen hadn't the faintest idea of how Orelia knew where she was going, but after an hour of quietly hurrying down forest paths, they emerged at the edge of the estate's open lawn. Only, it wasn't so open. Rows of tents dotted the lawn, a few men milling about between them. There seemed to be two distinct groups. One had been set up in a neat and orderly fashion with small, low-to-the-ground skins stretched over frames. The other was a bit more ramshackle in its lines, their shelters made of greased tarps.

"Bless it," Orelia spat, shrinking back within the woodline with Xellen. "That must be the villagers."

"Villagers?"

The knight nodded, pressing her arms together over her chest. "Nerinea's mother said the lord's men had pressed every man and boy in the village into service. It is a barbaric tactic to use untrained civilians as a front line to protect the more highly skilled soldiers behind them in a charge."

"Blessed Uaris, no." But Xellen could see by the grim set of Orelia's mouth that she was telling the truth. "We have to help them."

"I know." Chewing her lip, Orelia frowned in concentration, eyes flicking over the grounds. "I have an idea, but you aren't going to like it."

Xellen didn't like it, but, as Orelia pointed out, she didn't have any alternatives to offer. So she waited, hunkered in the shadow of a massive tree, for Orelia's plan to begin. It seemed to take an age, the only sounds after the knight slunk out of view were the distant, erratic murmur of voices and the infrequent calls from the menagerie of creatures she couldn't even name.

A shudder worked its way down her spine. She'd hoped to never see that beastly stone edifice again. At least this time it would definitely be the last. She shifted in the wet leaf litter and needles, brushing a beetle from her arm as she tried to be patient, but it seemed to be taking an age, and with every passing minute, she couldn't help but wonder if something had gone wrong.

And then, without warning, she saw a ripple of excitement roll through the tents on the lawn. People began to emerge from their tents, voices raising as they all pointed in the direction Orelia had gone, some running in the direction of the commotion. Creeping forward, Xellen strained to see around the heavy boughs of the pine, and felt her eyes widen.

Bright orange flames licked their way up the pines,

spitting whirling embers. How Orelia had managed to start such a large fire so quickly after the storm was a genuine mystery, but Xellen supposed it did its job. No one was looking as she stole out of the brush and quickly darted across the lawn into the shadow of the menagerie.

She waited a breath, looking about for anyone that might be headed her way, then sprang as high as she could into the air and fastened her long claws and talons in the stone. Dust and mortar rained down as she scurried up to the top of the wall, crouching at the edge to lean over and peer down into the menagerie. She could just make out three torchlights moving along the path towards the entrance, hopefully to go investigate Orelia's distraction.

Hopping down, she glided into the dark at the back of the menagerie, landing with hardly a sound. Now it was her turn to add to the chaos.

Moving quickly, she pulled the lever on the nearest cage, sending two striped horses galloping out with furious brays. The deafening shriek of a gryphon joined them shortly along with the strange crow of a beast with the fore parts of a horse and the hind parts of a rooster. One after the other, she set them free to whatever awaited them outside the cages they had been kept in against their will for the amusement of a man, until she came across a creature she recognized.

The manticore Orelia had released upon their escape lumbered free of its cage when she pulled the lever, fresh wounds weeping along its golden flanks.

But it was not the only creature kept within the cage.

A man's eyes found her in the dark, and with a painful, rasping breath, he called to her. "Agnolo?"

"You…" She crept closer, her nose wrinkling at the smell of blood and tainted flesh. A manticore's venom was an agonizing way to die.

"Remo…fed me to it," the dying man gasped, his face purple and slick with sweat. "I thought… I tried… I… I…" His mouth gaped open and closed like a fish plucked from the water, and Xellen felt a small sympathy for the fallen knight, though it was not nearly strong enough to wipe away her fury. Cirino may have helped them escape, but it was only after helping ensure her and Orelia's capture first. Pity, though. Pity she could spare him.

Crouching next to him, she set one of her sharp nails to his throat. "Uaris' wings gentle your passing into your next life," she prayed and pressed her nail into his skin.

Blood, hot and reeking of venom, gushed from the wound, quickly pooling around him. Reaching blindly, his hand found hers, squeezing tightly as he gawped up at her mutely, eyes round and white as the moon. She squeezed back, averting her eyes as his body slumped into the straw, eyes staring at nothing as his body twitched a final time, and fell still.

She held his hand a moment longer, until she was certain he wouldn't rise again, then gently placed it beside him.

There was a loud clank behind her, and she whirled to see the cage door slam shut. "No!" She launched herself at the bars, prying desperately, but the gate was unmoving.

"I knew it."

Her eyes snapped to the man standing with his hand on the lever, teeth bared white below his dark mustache in a sneer of a smile.

"I knew you'd be back. Agnolo never did know how to let matters lie. Always had to pry." Remo turned away, crossing to the cage opposite hers and taking the torch from the wall. "I was hoping I'd catch him, but I can wait. Your dog should come running soon. And then—" He lifted his sword, turning the blade to catch the firelight. "—I'll make sure that cur doesn't get up this time."

Xellen's heart plummeted. She was bait. And Orelia would leap into the trap with both feet the moment she saw Xellen.

Chapter Twenty-Four

Orelia ran through the trees as quickly as she dared, stopping here and there to kick over the thick bed of pine needles under bushes and at the bases of the trees to strike an ember into them. They were quick to kindle, the needles below dry and brittle from the long summer. She could hear the alarmed shouts behind her, bodies being roused from sleep. It was only too bad she couldn't have set the entire estate on fire.

She circled back to where she'd left Xellen, keeping to the shadows when there was a sudden burst of screams from the encampment of mercenaries. Darting behind a tree, she peered out in time to see a beast with the forebody of an eagle and the backend of a lion take to the air. She grinned. Things were going according to plan.

Now for the tricky part.

With a quick glance left and right for any guards or mercenaries, she bolted from her cover for the shadow of the menagerie, following it around to the entrance. She stopped again in the sheltering branches of an ornately shaped bush just as another creature came bursting out of the gates, scattering the guards who had been attempting to enter. Unnoticed, she slipped inside.

It was darker inside than she remembered, but the smell was the same. The smell of iron and shit and misery. She clutched the firestarter until the iron bit into her palm, a sneer of a smile crossing her lips as she went deeper into the menagerie.

"Xellen? Are you here?"

"Orelia? Watch out! Remo—"

A sudden glow of firelight threw Orelia's shadow in stark relief against the bars of a nearby cage where she could see Xellen pressed against the bars, her face a mask of horror. Pivoting, Orelia leapt back, a fine line of fire opening across her middle as her attacker's sword grazed her belly.

"I knew you'd be back, Agnolo," Remo snarled, the blaze of his torch casting demonic shadows across his face. His blade sang as it wove seamlessly through neat patterns, chasing Orelia back as she twisted and ducked to avoid the lethal edge. "You just can't help turning up where you don't belong."

"I'm here to stop you," Orelia sneered, spinning and making a grab for the lever. Her fingers had barely closed around it when there was a *crack* across the back of her head. Her vision flashed white, and the next thing she knew, she was on her knees, stars spinning through her vision.

"You couldn't even stop me from killing you," Remo's voice crawled into her ear.

Orelia lurched towards him with a snarl, ducking his blade as she bowled her shoulder into him. With a sound of disgust, Remo stumbled back until he caught his footing and flung his torch away to grab a fistful of Orelia's hair, wrenching her head back.

"You stupid—"

Xellen let out a cry of distress, and Orelia caught a glimpse of flames. Clamping her hand around Remo's wrist, she snapped her elbow up, catching the man squarely on his chin. With a snarled curse, Remo reared back and smashed her nose with his forehead. And then again.

The pain was blinding, tears springing to Orelia's eyes in an instant before he caught her across the jaw with another hard blow. She spun, knees buckling when he planted a boot solidly in the center of her back, throwing her to the floor.

She tried to get up, tried to lift her aching head, when a hand closed on her hip, flipping her over to face Remo's leering grin.

"Well, well." His eyes moved over her, settling on her bare chest. She tried to cover herself, coughing and choking on the blood from her broken nose. Sheathing his sword, he kicked her knees apart and knelt, forcing her thighs open with his.

A cold horror shot through Orelia's middle, and she scrambled backwards to get away. "No!"

The back of Remo's hand cracked across her cheek,

and her vision narrowed to a pinprick, her ears ringing.

"Look at this." A hand glided up her belly to cup her breast, fondling it roughly. "Your curse finally gave you what you wanted." He pinched her, the sharp pain bringing her vision back into focus. "You fucking monster."

"Orelia!"

Orelia's eyes swung towards the voice and saw the torch flying end over end towards them. Pushing herself up, she threw her arm up to try to catch it, but Remo was faster.

He snatched the torch out of the air, smiling triumphantly down at Orelia as he raised it above his head and swung.

With a desperate cry, Orelia snatched at the torch and by some miracle caught it—by the lit end. She screamed as the resin covering her hand ignited in a crackling burst, but she didn't let go.

"You—Ack!" Whatever insult Remo had been about to hurl was stifled as Orelia grabbed him by the face, pushing him away as she fought for the torch. His hand clamped around her wrist, pulling it away from his face as he sat up above her, squeezing until the bones grated painfully, but Orelia could hardly feel it through the agony of her other hand. He let out a snarl of vehement curses, wrenching the torch from her fingers, and reared back to strike her.

"No!" A clump of flaming hay struck the side of Remo's head, sending a spray of scalding embers across his face and neck. He howled in pain, swatting at the biting orange embers only for Orelia to drop to her elbow and snap her leg up to catch him across the face.

He went over with a ragged cry, the torch clattering from his grip, and Orelia quickly got her feet and snatched it up in her good hand. She whirled on Remo, raising her arm to strike him before she thought better of it and ran for the lever to the cage.

"Get back here!" he snarled, but she'd already released the mechanism as she turned to face him. Blood poured down his face, the skin below his left eye hanging in a bloody flap. "I was going to just kill you before," he threatened, drawing his blade as he advanced. "Now I think I'll take my time."

He sprang forward, sword carving through the air, and Orelia shifted her grip on her torch to parry the mighty blow, when a golden shadow collided with the man, sending him sprawling.

Xellen stood tall, wings spread, and turned eyes alight with fury to Orelia. She smiled, fierce and terrifying and more beautiful than any woman Orelia had ever seen, and she found herself smiling back.

They moved in unison, Xellen striking at Remo with her dangerous talons while Orelia swooped in to steal the blade right from the man's fingers, delivering another kick to his bloodied face. Throwing the torch away, she wrapped both hands around the hilt of the sword and with a scream that encompassed all of her rage and disgust and pain, she drove the blade into the man's back.

He let out a short, pained sound, limbs flailing

briefly like a bug pinned to a card before Orelia tore the blade free again. He wheezed, his eyes finding hers, blazing with hatred as bloody foam spilled out of his mouth before he sagged against the stones.

Orelia waited, certain he would somehow rise to keep fighting, but he only lay there as the pool of blood beneath him slowly spread across the mosaic tile. He was dead. He was finally, truly dead.

Her sword clattered to the ground as a sob tore its way free and she sank to her knees. It was over. It was finally over.

Chapter Twenty-Five

O relia!" Xellen caught the knight in her arms, cradling her against her chest. Gods, she had never been so scared in her life, certain she'd been about to watch her love die again. But there was no time to dawdle. There surely must be other soldiers coming.

"Can you stand?" When Orelia didn't answer, Xellen cupped her cheek and turned the knight's gaze up to her, away from that rotten man. As terrible as it was, she couldn't deny the righteous satisfaction she felt seeing Remo dead.

"We've got to go," she whispered urgently, pressing a kiss to Orelia's forehead, the only place on her face not covered in blood. "Come on."

Orelia nodded meekly, then seemed to shake off whatever spell had come over her. She struggled to her feet, cradling her injured hand close. Xellen tried not to look at it, tried not to smell the awful stench of burnt flesh and feathers. The skin had cracked and blistered, even blackened in places, and Xellen wondered if Orelia would ever fly now.

She shook her head, looping her arm around Orelia's back and starting towards the front of the menagerie. The matriarch would know what to do if they could only get back.

"Wait," Orelia croaked, staggering to a stop. "The torch. We have to finish this."

"Orelia, you're hurt. We need to go."

But the knight shrugged out of her hold. "Not without finishing what we came for." She took up the torch in her good hand, hissing as her injured hand brushed her leg.

Xellen glanced towards the shouts and cries of battle coming from the front of the menagerie, then thrust out her hand. "Let me take it then."

They followed the path towards the exit in the direction Xellen had been going, stopping at each and every cage to release any occupants they found and to set fire to the straw and any structures within. By the time they reached the double doors, the menagerie was thick with black smoke and the roar of flames.

Xellen stopped as they reached the last cage, watching the enclosure go up in flames, as all of it was engulfed in a conflagration. It felt good. No one else would ever be caged here for any lord or mercenary to leer at.

Tossing the torch aside, she wrapped an arm around Orelia again, and led them out into the night.

To her surprise, the initial chaos the fires and beasts

from the menagerie had caused had been joined by a full out melee with soldiers in red and white heraldry.

"That's the Crown's colors," Orelia said, her eyes panning over the battle. "They came. My letter… They came." Her voice hitched, and Xellen tightened her arm at Orelia's back.

"You did it," she reassured her, eyes darting nervously over the clashing soldiers, all too aware it would only take one of them to—

She froze, her gaze locked on a man not fifty feet from them, his bow drawn and pointed straight at them. A hundred thoughts crowded her mind all at once— regrets for her wasted youth in a loveless marriage, sunny days spent on the shore of a lake, the terror of being captured by vicious men. But most poignantly, she regretted she wouldn't have more time with Orelia after everything they went through. She only hoped she might see the knight again on Uaris' far shores.

And then the man's eyes switched over her head, and his expression softened in surprise, his bow drooping. Xellen felt Orelia stiffen at her side, breath catching in a soft gasp.

"Master?" the knight breathed.

The man looked between the two of them, expression turning thoughtful and then grim, before, with a slight incline of his head, he deliberately turned his back to them.

Xellen let out her breath, fighting back tears of sheer relief. "Uaris be praised," she whispered, looking up at Orelia to find tears streaming down the knight's face.

In spite of her tears, she laughed a little as they turned away, making haste towards the woods as the first fingers of dawn began to lighten the sky. "He recognized me."

Xellen's arm tightened at her back. "We'd better not press our luck with the others."

Orelia gave another weak laugh. "We might just need it to get back to the flock."

Xellen brushed the remark off, but she couldn't help silently fretting how she might get Orelia back to the roost. She supposed she could hide the knight amongst the sea caves again and go fetch help from the roost. Her wings ached with exhaustion already, but she steeled herself. They were nearly free now. They only had to make it back to the rock, and they could put all of this behind them. She would make it there and back if she had to swim the last hundred yards. For Orelia. For them.

<hr>

Dawn was shining hazily through the smoky air by the time Xellen and Orelia made it to the cliffs again. Squinting through the murk, Orelia swore she could just make out the yellow glow of the burning ship still out at sea. It was enough to bring a wan smile to her face.

Unfortunately, climbing down the narrow, winding goat path proved to be more difficult than ascending had been. The knight's hand and nose had begun throbbing in earnest, and her legs trembled with every step downward. Whenever she felt herself slowing or began to think of suggesting they rest, she forced herself to remember that this had been her idea in the first place. If she faltered, Xellen would stay there with her, even if it meant they both were captured or killed by the soldiers behind them. Setting her teeth, she swore a silent oath that she would make it back to the harpies' rock, for Xellen, if for no one or nothing else.

But when they finally reached the bottom, Orelia collapsed onto a fallen boulder, mopping the sweat from her forehead.

"May I see your hand?" Xellen asked, taking a seat beside her.

Orelia nearly said no. She'd gotten a brief glimpse of it earlier and while she was no healer, she knew enough about wounds to know this was a bad one. At Xellen's gentle, imploring look, she held it out for the harpy to see, grimacing when Xellen's face went bloodless.

"Saveone knows a lot of remedies. We'll have her look at it when we get back."

"I don't think there is a remedy for this." She retracted her hand, her fingers twitching briefly as she tried to open them, sending a flash of white hot pain radiating up her arm that threatened to turn her stomach.

A hand settled against her lower back, rubbing soothing circles against her skin. "Did he hurt you anywhere else?"

Orelia shook her head gingerly. "Just my nose, I think. Shouldn't—"

A face surfaced silently from the water, grinning to

show long pointed teeth. "You're back," Nerinea hummed, her voice a sonorous thrum against Orelia's chest. Her eyes slid to Xellen, her nose crinkling in amusement. "Both of you."

"Can you take Orelia back to the roost?" Xellen cut in before Orelia could find the words.

"Certainly. I've had my fill of fun, but what about you?"

"I'll fly."

"Suit yourself." The bottomless black eyes of the siren fixed on Orelia again as she slunk forwards into the shallows, her body no more than a swaying shadow beneath the water. "Come here little bird."

Accepting Xellen's help, Orelia waded out into the water, shivering as the cold lapped up her calves, her knees, her thighs, until it closed around her hips. It wasn't until Nerinea's arms wrapped around her and pulled her into the water and the salty water touched her ruined hand that she realized her mistake.

It was like a branding iron thrust into her flesh and twisted. Her vision flashed white, and she convulsed with a scream, cold water flooding her mouth and nose, setting her lungs aflame. And then there was nothing but an endless black nothing.

Chapter Twenty-Six

Orelia awoke disorientated. She was in a strange, yet somehow familiar room with no knowledge of how she got there or why it wasn't Xellen's nest. She was tired and her body felt wrung out, but the throbbing pain of before had subsided. She turned her head and caught sight of the table next to the fireplace, and the old woman perched in the chair peeling vegetables. Near her, curled up beneath a worn quilt in front of the fire, was Xellen, fast asleep.

"How—" The word came out a ragged croak, and Maura looked up at her.

"Well, welcome back," the woman said, leaning to shake Xellen awake. "Gave us all quite a fright."

"Back?"

Xellen jerked awake, eyes searching wildly until they landed on Orelia. Gasping, she threw off her quilt and knelt at the bedside. "Lia!"

Rolling onto her side, Orelia scooped the harpy up

into a one-armed embrace, squeezing her until she was sure she was real. "You're all right?"

"Yes. Yes. I'm fine," Xellen assured her, showering her shoulders and neck with kisses before drawing back. The harpy looked well but for a few healing bruises and scrapes along her cheek and forehead, her curly hair a wild tangle from sleep. Laying her cheek on the mattress next to Orelia, Xellen pushed a lock of yellow hair from the knight's eyes, stroking along her jaw. "You wouldn't wake up. Maura said it was the shock of everything."

"You took a fever," the older woman said, creakily getting up from her chair. "Tended you best I know how, but I'm no healer."

Orelia frowned as she absorbed their words. "How long have I..." Her voice cracked, her mouth dry and tacky. "May I... Water?"

"Here." Maura ladled out a fresh cup from the barrel near the fire and waited as Orelia pushed up onto her elbow. But as she went to sit up, she noticed something wrong with the way her hand pressed into the mattress. That was when she finally noticed her hand.

She stared at the place it had once been, now nothing more than a swath of bandages. She tried to move her fingers or even her wrist, but the club of bandages remained unmoved.

"I saved what I could of it," the older woman said. "There wasn't much left."

"It'll be all right," Xellen said quickly, reaching to draw Orelia's eyes back to her with a hand on her cheek. "I won't leave you."

Orelia's frown deepened, the uncanniness of her ruined hand subsumed by confusion. "Why would you leave me?"

"Because that's what the rest of them did," Maura said, holding out the water. "Here. Drink up."

Orelia stared between the two, trying to comprehend just what she was being told. "The harpies…?"

"Left," Maura confirmed, and Orelia could see by the pain in Xellen's eyes that it was true.

"After they saw the fires and caught wind of the King's Army in the area, they decided to leave and join the others in safety," Xellen said in a small voice, turning to take the water from Maura. "They asked me to go with them, but I… I couldn't leave you."

Tears leaked from Orelia's eyes and down her cheeks as the full weight of Xellen's words hit her. They'd been left—Xellen had been left by the people she had called family for years before Orelia came along. And it was her fault. Orelia was the one who had been so stubbornly persistent about pursuing Remo and trying to single handedly bring down his and the Lord Boni's plot. She, a single, inexperienced knight against two armies. A crippled hand was a small payment for her arrogance in comparison.

"Oh no, please." Xellen set the cup aside and rose to her knees, cupping Orelia's face and brushing her tears away with her thumbs. "Don't cry."

"You should have gone. I made my choice. They're your family."

Xellen shook her head, leaning forward to gently kiss Orelia. "Did you forget? You're my family too."

"But—"

"Shush. If you think I was going to walk away and leave you behind again, you have a lot more to learn about me, Orelia Sanctis." She kissed Orelia again, and this time, Orelia leaned into it, relief and guilt all mixed up together with a fluttering thrill in her chest.

Her throat closed up, eyes welling again as their lips parted. Wordlessly she gripped Xellen's shoulder.

The harpy must have sensed what she couldn't say. "I love you, Orelia," she murmured, pulling the knight down into an embrace. "I always have."

"I love you, too," Orelia blubbered, pressing her face into her friend's shoulder as a sob worked its way up and out of her. "I'm so sorry."

"There's nothing to be sorry about," Maura cut in, settling in her chair at the fire again. "One of them is still flapping around out there. I'm sure she knows where they're going."

"What?" Orelia peered at Xellen, whose cheeks turned rosy.

"Florys. She stayed behind to guide us."

Orelia sniffled, sinking into Xellen's embrace as the harpy stroked her hair. "I can't fly."

The old woman chuffed. "Neither can I. You'll just have to make the journey the same way us mortals do. I might even have a boat somewhere abouts that you could use if you were in need and a daughter that could use a pair of friends like you."

A sea voyage with a siren and the love of her life. Orelia tilted her head up to Xellen, who gazed down at her in steady, sweet adoration. Even the chance to see her face looking back at her like that for whatever days Uaris had graced her with was more than she had before, and it was more than worth whatever hardship they might face navigating unfamiliar waters to find their family..

"As long as you'll have me," she said at last, winding her fingers through Xellen's hair to pull her down into another kiss.

Xellen laughed, her mouth crushing against Orelia's. "For as long as you'll love me."

About The Author

SAM THORNE is one half of the pen behind Thorne and Ivey. An ace spectrum nonbinary with an eclectic resume of skills and interests—including ones gained from their careers as a wildland firefighter and microbiologist—they bring an interesting perspective to the creative process. When not writing either their own projects or cowritten ones with their friend and writing partner Lauren Ivey, they spend their time doting on their cat, Midna, watching terrible horror flicks, and playing board games

 Thorne.And.Ivey

ThorneAndIvey.com